TALES OF MYSTERY & T

General Editor: David Stuart Davies

SHERLOCK HOLMES AND
THE HENTZAU AFFFAIR

SHERLOCK HOLMES
AND THE
HENTZAU AFFAIR

by David Stuart Davies

WORDSWORTH EDITIONS

2

Readers who are interested in other titles from
Wordsworth Editions are invited to visit our website at
www.wordsworth-editions.com

For our latest list and a full mail-order service contact
Bibliophile Books, 5 Thomas Road, London E14 7BN
Tel: +44 0207 515 9222 Fax: +44 0207 538 4115
e-mail: orders@bibliophilebooks.com

This edition published 2007 by
Wordsworth Editions Limited
8B East Street, Ware, Hertfordshire SG12 9HJ

ISBN 978 1 84022 548 8

© Wordsworth Editions Limited 2007

Wordsworth® is a registered trademark of
Wordsworth Editions Limited

All rights reserved. This publication may
not be reproduced, stored in a retrieval system or
transmitted in any form or by any means, electronic,
mechanical, photocopying, recording or otherwise,
without the prior permission of the publishers.

Typeset in Great Britain by Chrissie Madden
Printed by Clays Ltd, St Ives plc

CONTENTS

SHERLOCK HOLMES AND
THE HENTZAU AFFAIR

FOR ROGER JOHNSON
friend and fellow Sherlockian,
whose observations and advice
were a great help in writing
this book

PREFACE

The events related in this adventure which I had the privilege to share with my friend, Sherlock Holmes, the best and wisest man whom I have ever known, took place in 1895. I knew at the time of recording the affair in my private notebooks that the world would have to wait some time before the full story could be told.

However, I did not realise how our world would change so dramatically. With the turn of this century came the growing unrest in Europe, finally climaxing in the assassinations in Sarajevo, precipitating the war to end all wars. The achievements of old Europe in the 19th century had been without parallel in human history, but now it was on its deathbed, partly through the mistakes and weaknesses of its leaders and partly through the only half-understood destructive powers with which its own achievements had endowed it. There was a strong and, I consider, a false concept fostered by the young idealists that progress was only possible through destruction of the old. They were willing, even anxious, in a supreme moment of blindness to leap forward into a new and fundamentally different future. It meant the passing of the age of the monarch: Europe was thrown into the melting pot and old ideologies and dynasties were destroyed by the flames of war, never to rise again. Among those consumed in this terrible conflagration was the Kingdom of Ruritania, the main backdrop for this adventure.

As the smoke of conflict cleared in 1918, I knew there were no longer any constraints for me to keep this story secret, but even so, something within me told me that it was still not the right time to publish this memoir. So I placed it, together with many other unrecorded cases of Sherlock Holmes, in a travel-worn and battered tin dispatch box in the vaults of Cox & Co at Charing Cross. I have decreed that fifty years after my death, when all the actors in this particular drama are long dead, the story of the Hentzau affair may be finally set before the world.

JOHN H. WATSON, M.D.
London, 6th May, 1919

Chapter One
Colonel Sapt

I have often reflected that of the many investigations carried out by my friend, the celebrated detective, Mr Sherlock Holmes, those which had the most dramatic openings often led on to even more dramatic conclusions. Certainly no case bears more proof of this observation than that I am about to relate, one that placed the future peace of Europe in jeopardy and very nearly cost us our lives.

Little did Holmes and I know of our impending adventure on that day in 1895 as we took an early evening stroll in Hyde Park. The day had been one of inaction for my friend and, as the atmosphere of our sitting room had grown denser with the dark fumes of his shag tobacco, I was unable to stand it any longer and prevailed upon him to take the air. Reluctantly, he agreed.

It is with a certain irony that the change of seasons can be observed more readily and with more apparent dramatic change by dwellers in the great metropolis than is seen in the sleepy shires. London's fine parks and tree-lined thoroughfares which thread their way through the capital wear the seasons like emblems: the stark blacks and greys of winter; the fresh greens and budding pinks of spring; the lushness of the summer; and the amber variants of autumn. A walk in London at whatever time of year always brings one into direct contact with the capricious face of Mother Nature.

The summer that year had been glorious; but yet a few weeks into September, the trees had begun to glow with cupreous tints. As we strolled past the leaden Serpentine, I observed the absence of the smart row-boats so popular in the summer months – another sure sign that the bright year was fading. Turning our faces to home, we were already aware of the oncoming chill of evening as the breeze stiffened, rustling the brittle leaves.

'Despite all the power that man can muster, Watson, he is power-less against time and the change of the seasons: they are relentless.

We may be, as Shakespeare has it, "the paragon of animals", but we are still the slaves of time,' my friend remarked with a melancholy air.

Holmes had been in a silent and morose mood all day and it seemed the dying season had increased his *taedium vitae*. As his close companion, I was no stranger to these fits of depression. His brain was such a finely wrought instrument that it was highly tuned to external sensations. I also realised that it was not just the unstoppable, headlong rush of time that darkened my friend's spirits; it was because he had no case on hand to occupy and challenge his incredible mind.

As we turned from Oxford Street towards Baker Street, the lamps were being lit; even the cabs that rattled down the cobbles had their carriage lamps aglow, little amber beacons to attract the customers.

Holmes and I had naturally lapsed into silence and each was lost in his own thoughts when out of the growing dusk I saw a face that I knew, looming towards me. It belonged to a friend of Peterson, the commissionaire, whom I had treated for a bout of pneumonia when Holmes had been out of town on one of his discreet investigations. The man, Cobb by name, was of lean appearance with a high-domed forehead and finely-chiselled aquiline nose, on the bridge of which was a carefully balanced pair of pince-nez. He had the look of a down-at-heel clergyman or academic. However, I knew him to be a cellar man at the Rose & Crown, a hostelry in Covent Garden much frequented by the porters.

As he approached he recognised me and, giving a surprised yell, grabbed me by the hand, shaking it vigorously. 'Hello, Doctor Watson,' he cried.

I smiled and nodded.

'As you can see, I'm hale and hearty now!'

'I'm pleased to hear it,' I said.

With that brief exchange we parted company, he, no doubt, hurrying off to his place of work. This chance meeting, however, had given me an idea.

'Now then, Holmes,' I said, turning to my silent companion, 'what can you tell me about that fellow?'

My friend looked at me with raised eyebrows and then gave a short laugh. I knew why he was amused. He had immediately seen through my little ploy to divert his mind from its melancholic track.

'Well,' said Holmes, still smiling, 'apart from the fact that you have treated him at one time in your medical career, that he works as a cellarman in a West End public house, probably the Rose and Crown, that he is neglectful of his health, has served in the army at one time and that he is a singularly unsuccessful gambler, I can tell you nothing.'

I stared at him for a moment in sheer amazement and then we both burst out laughing.

'Holmes,' I said at length, 'I can easily see how you deduced he was a one-time patient of mine, but as to the other details . . . Well, I'm at a loss to see how you can possibly know these things.'

Holmes pursed his lips. 'Really, Watson,' said he, 'you will have me play this game?'

'No game, I assure you. I am genuinely mystified by your ass-ertions.'

'Oh, very well,' he sighed somewhat impatiently, but I could tell from his manner that he found this little exercise entertaining. 'This is how I see the matter: the fellow hails you and refers to his health; obviously you have treated him for some ailment and, since you are no longer in practice, your ministration must have been made at the request of someone local who knows your expertise. This would most likely by Mrs Hudson or Peterson, the commissionaire. The patient does not seem the kind of acquaintance our landlady fosters, so probability points to Peterson. Now, although this fellow has had recourse to call in a doctor recently – so recently that he remembers your face in the street at dusk – he fails to wear appropriate clothing for the chill of the evening: hence he is neglectful of his health. On the subject of his clothes: they gave off a strong odour of beer and the knees of his trousers were badly worn. These facts imply he is employed on licensed premises in a manual capacity. The job of a cellarman very naturally presents itself. As a friend of Peterson, his place of work is likely to be our commissionaire friend's regular drinking haunt, which is, I believe, the Rose & Crown on Henrietta Street. Like you, Watson, an old army man rarely learns new tricks. His handkerchief . . . '

'Tucked up his sleeve?'

'Exactly.'

'And the unsuccessful gambling?'

'When I see a copy of the *Sporting Life* sticking out of a man's pocket, it is safe to assume he is a gambler and, if that man is shabbily dressed, there is clear evidence of his lack of success in this pursuit.'

'Splendid, Holmes, splendid!' I cried in genuine admiration of my friend's remarkable analysis.

'I'm glad you think so,' he replied with little enthusiasm. 'It may seem inspired to you, but such an exercise is elementary to me, my dear Watson, and therefore it makes no real demand on my deductive processes. My brain craves a real challenge, one that will use its capacity to the full. While this reasoning machine is idle,' and he tapped his temple with his forefinger, 'the whole man suffers: the dust of commonplace settles and deadens the spirit. However,' he continued, with a softening of his stern features, 'I do appreciate the thought behind your little ruse.'

Just as I was about to reply, my attention was taken by the deafening clatter of hooves and loud cries as a hansom cab thundered by us at speed, the passenger, a large, thick-set man, leaning out, urging the driver on.

'Halloa, what have we here?' murmured Holmes, as the cab shuddered and rattled to a halt outside our own chambers. The passenger leapt out and, thrusting some coins into the driver's hand, proceeded to rap loudly on our door with his stick. Holmes laughed out loud. 'A client, my boy. This visitor could well be the ladder by which we are able to climb out of the dreary pit.'

As he spoke the man was pushing his way past a somewhat bewildered Mrs Hudson.

'Whatever it is,' I said, 'the matter is urgent.'

'Let us hope so,' replied Holmes, rubbing his hands with glee.

By the time we had reached our door the blinds of our sitting room had been drawn, against which I could see the silhouette of our visitor passing to and fro in an agitated manner.

Holmes was smiling in his tight-lipped fashion. 'Where there is such vacillation, Watson, there is also a very troubled mind.'

On entering 221b, a worried-looking Mrs Hudson met us in the hall. 'There is a gentleman here to see you, Mr Holmes,' she said in hushed, conspiratorial tones. 'He seemed very perturbed and was determined to await your return, so I took the liberty of showing him to your sitting room.'

'Quite right too, Mrs Hudson,' approved Holmes, mounting the stairs with enthusiasm.

As we entered the room our visitor, who was still in the process of pacing the floor, turned abruptly to face us. He was short and stoutly built, with a large bullet-shaped head, the hair of which was close cropped. A bristly grey moustache adorned his upper lip. He had the bearing and appearance of an old soldier.

'Which of you is Sherlock Holmes, the private investigator?' He barked the question at us and, although he spoke in perfect English, there was an unmistakeable trace of accent in his voice.

'I am Sherlock Holmes and this is my friend and associate, Doctor Watson.'

Our visitor clicked his heels and gave a curt bow. 'I am Colonel Sapt in the service of King Rudolf the Fifth of Ruritania.'

'Indeed,' said Holmes urbanely, throwing off his outer clothes. 'Do take a seat, Colonel Sapt, Mrs Hudson will serve tea shortly.'

Sapt's eyes twinkled icily in his pale, strained face, glistening with perspiration in the gaslight. He slapped his leather gloves down on the table with irritation. 'I am afraid I have no time for your English niceties, Mr Holmes. I am here in your country on a secret errand of the utmost importance. Circumstances have conspired to place me in a position where I need help desperately. There is no time to lose. The purpose of my mission prevents me from approaching the authorities for aid. So, having heard of your reputation, I come to you as my last resort.'

Holmes looked keenly at Sapt. 'I earn my bread and cheese by taking on those problems that, for whatever reason, the official police are unable to handle,' he said, sweeping a pile of newspapers from the basket chair on to the floor. 'As for English niceties, Colonel, I must assure you that in this instance they are purely practical. I want you relaxed and refreshed so that you are able to relate in full and accurate detail the causes of your problem. If I am to help you, this is essential. Now, sir, do take this chair by the fire. A rushed and garbled tale will hinder, rather than assist, a swift solution to the matter on which you wish to consult me.'

Sapt gave a grunt of impatience, took a few uncertain steps forward and then, to our great surprise, with rolling eyes and flailing arms, he crashed to the floor, prostrate and insensible upon our bearskin rug.

Chapter Two

The royal impostor

For an instant Holmes and I stared in silent amazement at the inert figure before us; then, while my friend hurried with a cushion for his head and brandy for his lips, I knelt and loosened his collar and felt his pulse where the stream of life flowed erratically.

'What is it, Watson?'

'He has simply fainted. Probably his strong emotions overcame him.'

'I am perfectly all right,' croaked our visitor, his heavy eyes flickering open in that solid, white face, seamed with lines of trouble. Holmes held the brandy to his lips and he drank. 'A momentary weakness, I assure you, gentlemen,' Sapt said, pulling himself into a sitting position. 'I shall be myself again within a moment. However, I would appreciate another sip of brandy; it is most invigorating.' The stern features softened and a thin smile touched his lips.

Fifteen minutes later Colonel Sapt was seated by our fireside, drinking a cup of tea and apparently none the worse for wear.

Holmes was sitting opposite him, relaxed in his mouse-coloured dressing gown, puffing on his old black clay pipe. 'Now, sir,' said he, 'I should be pleased to hear your story, and pray be precise as to detail.'

Sapt put his cup down, leaned forward and then hesitated for a moment, as though to clear his mind – then he began. 'First, with regard to what I am about to tell you, I must bind you, as gentlemen of honour, to the utmost secrecy.'

'You need have no fear on that account,' Holmes assured him. 'This will not be the first time that Watson and I have been privy to the secrets of a royal household. Our discretion is guaranteed.'

I gave a nod of agreement.

'Thank you, gentlemen,' acknowledged Sapt. 'This matter is of such a grave and delicate nature that public knowledge would bring ruin and disgrace to the House of Elfberg. Now, in order to acquaint you fully with this desperate business, I must begin by referring to events that took place some three years ago.'

'Three years ago!' I exclaimed, unable to contain my surprise.

Holmes sighed impatiently. 'If you find this absolutely necessary, Colonel Sapt, please be brief and to the point.'

Sapt's eyes flickered angrily for a second before he commenced his narrative. 'On the day before the Coronation of King Rudolf the Fifth, which was to take place in the Ruritanian capital of Strelsau, the King and I, and another trusted member of the Royal Household, Fritz von Tarlenheim, had spent the day hunting in the forest near the town of Zenda, some fifty miles from the capital. It was intended that after this day of relaxation for the King, he would spend the night in the royal hunting lodge on the edge of the forest before travelling to Strelsau the next day for his Coronation. While in the woods we encountered an Englishman, Rudolf Rassendyll, who was holidaying in the district. We were all struck by the amazing resemblance he had to the King. In fact, we found out later that the Rassendylls are descendants of the illegitimate son of Rudolf the Second, who, as a young prince, visited the English Court, where he met and wooed a married lady, the wife of the fifth Earl of Burlesdon. The Prince eventually left England under a cloud after fighting a duel with the Earl. Two months later the lady gave birth to a son.'

'Please, spare me the social history,' sighed Holmes wearily.

Sapt took no notice of Holmes's interruption and carried on unabashed. 'Apparently every so often the Elfberg features – the long, straight nose and thick dark red hair – manifest themselves in a Rassendyll. Rassendyll is the family name of the Burlesdons. This chance meeting in the woods with the latest of the Rassendylls to bear the hereditary characteristics was to prove a fateful blessing.

'The King was so taken with the novelty of seeing his "twin", as it were, that he insisted the young Rassendyll should dine with us that evening at the lodge. The Englishman, who was visiting Ruritania for the purpose of seeing the Coronation, was readily agreeable to this suggestion.

'The evening was disastrous. Both Fritz and I could see the King was drinking far too freely, unheeding our pleas for moderation, and the necessity for a clear head for the following day. The truth is, Mr Holmes, the King is a weak-willed man, lacking both the discipline and sense of duty required by his exalted position.'

I could see that it was hard for Sapt to admit these failings of his monarch, but, although I had only known this man but a short time, I believed he was telling the truth.

'Towards the end of the evening Josef, the servant who had been attending on us, set down an old wicker-covered flagon before the King, saying it was a gift from the Duke of Strelsau, Black Michael, the King's brother.' Sapt shook his head sadly. 'I can remember Rudolf's response to this day: "Out with the cork, Josef," he cried. "Hang him! Did he think I'd flinch from his bottle?" '

'Michael was a rival for the throne?' asked Holmes, leaning back in his chair with his eyes closed.

'Indeed he was. Black Michael was a jealous and evil man who bore Rudolf nothing but ill-will, but, despite protestations from Fritz and myself, the bottle was tasted by the King. Then, with a solemnity born of the hour and his own condition, he looked round on us: "Gentlemen, my friends, Rudolf, my cousin, everything is yours to the half of Ruritania. But ask me not for a single drop of this divine bottle, which I will drink to the health of that – that sly knave, my brother, Black Michael." And then he seized the bottle and drained it dry.'

Sapt paused momentarily to light a small cigar. 'We all slept heavily that night, but none more so than the King. In the morning there was no waking him; he remained in a kind of deep stupor.'

'Aha,' exclaimed Holmes, his eyes flashing open, 'The wine had been drugged.'

'Exactly. It was Black Michael's plan to prevent the King being crowned. I knew that if Rudolf did not mount the throne that day, he never would. Imagine it, gentlemen, the whole nation crowding the streets of the capital, half the army in attendance with Black Michael at their head: Rudolf must be there. It was certain we could not send word that the King was ill: the people knew of his "illnesses" all too well. He had been "ill" once too often.'

'You assumed that Black Michael planned to take Rudolf's place at the Coronation?' I asked.

'I was convinced of it, Doctor. He had been courting the popularity of the people with this in mind. The whole state was on holiday, fired with coronation fever; a monarch had to be crowned that day. And here was Michael, smiling sweetly, shaking his head sadly at his brother's failings; surely he could be persuaded . . . Bah!' Sapt banged the arm of his chair. 'It makes my blood boil even now to think of it and how close that blackguard came to wearing the crown.'

'How was it prevented? Did the King recover in time?' I enquired.

'Sapt shook his head. 'No, sir, he did not.'

'You had Rassendyll impersonate the King,' said Holmes quietly.

Sapt gave a start. 'How the devil . . . ?'

Holmes smiled. 'It is the only logical solution to the dilemma. There is a king about to be crowned who has been drugged and is in no way capable of carrying out his duties – while on the other hand there is an Englishman who bears an amazing resemblance to him. You had no choice other than to persuade Rassendyll to take the King's place.'

'It was a dangerous risk, but, as you say, there was no alternative. After some persuasion from Fritz and myself, Rassendyll reluctantly agreed.'

'So, technically speaking,' observed Holmes, 'King Rudolf has never been crowned.'

Sapt's features clouded. 'I am afraid not, Mr Holmes,' he admitted gravely. 'I will not bother you with the detail of how, in that short time available to us, we coached Rassendyll on the etiquette of the Ruritanian Court and on the past life, family tastes and character of the King, as well as those duties that were expected of him during the Coronation; suffice it to say that Rassendyll behaved wonderfully and fooled everyone.'

'Everyone except Black Michael.'

'Yes, except Michael and his treacherous accomplice, Rupert of Hentzau.' Sapt allowed himself a little chuckle. 'Michael nearly exploded with rage when he came face to face with Rassendyll in the Cathedral, but there was nothing he could say or do without exposing his own treachery. He had to stand by impotently as his brother's impostor was crowned King of Ruritania. However, the greatest test for the understudy that day was a meeting with Princess Flavia, the King's betrothed. She was not fully deceived. She observed subtle differences in Rassendyll, more in his behaviour than in his appearance, but these changes impressed her and she saw them as improvements rather than discrepancies, wrongly assuming that, at last, Rudolf was behaving like a king – which, indeed, Rassendyll did. He was every inch an Elfberg.'

'Presumably there were some troublesome consequences resulting from Rassendyll's substitution?' commented Holmes.

'After the Coronation festivities, Rassendyll and I returned to the hunting lodge under cover of darkness. The plan was for the Englishman to head for the border, while the King and I returned to

Strelsau. However, on reaching the lodge we found Josef, who had been left in charge of His Majesty, murdered – a crimson gash across his throat. The King was gone!'

Holmes raised a quizzical brow. 'Black Michael.'

'Yes. Damn him. A group of men led by Rupert of Hentzau had snatched the King and delivered him to Michael's stronghold, the Castle of Zenda. He knew, of course, that we could not raise the alarm without publicly exposing our own action – placing an impostor on the throne of Ruritania.'

'So Rassendyll had to continue playing the role of King.'

'There was no other alternative. I will not weary you with a full account of the events that followed; suffice it to say, Rassendyll, brave fellow that he was, did not flinch from his duty. If only he had been the rightful heir! He was far more fitted for the role than Rudolf. Little did I think then that my idle thoughts . . . '

Sapt's words faded away and he stared into the dancing flames of our fire, momentarily lost in thought; then with a brief shake of his grey head, he resumed his narrative.

'One unforeseen outcome of Rassendyll's continued impersonation was that he and Flavia fell in love. Still believing he was Rudolf, a changed and improved Rudolf, she saw in him all she had ever wanted in her betrothed. Rassendyll's warmth and nobility captured her heart, while her supreme beauty and natural grace broke down any reserve he may have felt. It was a natural blossoming of true love. They made a happy and honourable couple.'

'Quite,' said Holmes with the faintest trace of irony in his voice. I knew that he, with his regard for cold-hearted reason and a strong distaste for what he considered were the weaker emotions, would find this talk of romance irritating and irrelevant. 'Tell me, Colonel,' he continued briskly, his hooded eyes flashing with a keen brilliance, 'how was this little dilemma of the kidnapped King resolved – as resolved it must have been? There has been no word of scandal or up-heaval in the Ruritanian Court that I can remember for many a year.'

'Indeed, Mr Holmes, King Rudolf was eventually rescued. With a picked body of soldiers, we surprised the Castle of Zenda in the dead of night. What bloodshed and mishap there was! But, thank the stars, our monarch was restored to us unharmed. Black Michael, however, in a fatal quarrel with Rupert of Hentzau was dispatched by the villain, who then, with the Devil's own luck, escaped all injury and fled to the hills.

'Rassendyll had one final meeting with Flavia, when she learnt the truth. The secret, thus shared, seemed to increase the deep regard they held for each other and sealed their undying love. However, duty controls so many of our lives: it was Rassendyll's duty to relinquish his role and leave Ruritania at speed, while it was Flavia's duty to be true to her country and take her place alongside the rightful heir to the throne. And this is what happened. Rassendyll returned home to England and the King, having recovered from his ordeal, married Flavia within the month . . . '

'And all was well with the world,' said Holmes, who rose from his chair with impatience and began pacing the room. 'Until now. Three years later events have occurred that have forced you to visit England on a mission of great urgency, a mission that is already threatened with failure.'

Sapt nodded his head in agreement.

'So at last we are getting to the heart of the matter,' Holmes announced. He flung himself back down in his chair and, extracting a small coal from the fire with the tongs, began to relight his pipe. For a few moments his face was obscured by thick puffs of grey smoke and then he addressed our visitor again. 'Now, Colonel Sapt, do tell us what your problem is and how you think I can help you.'

Clasping his hands very tightly in a nervous gesture, Sapt looked keenly at my friend. 'Very well. I will now turn to recent events which are intimately connected with those I have just related and which place the whole future of Ruritania on the brink of disaster.'

Chapter Three
The Blues

The autumnal wind had picked up somewhat since we had returned to our rooms and now it shook our windows with a moaning force, as though attempting to gain entry. The fire danced erratically in the grate, the flames caught by an errant draught from the chimney. However, Holmes and I had no thoughts of the weather as we listened intently to our visitor from Ruritania.

Holmes appeared relaxed, sitting back in his chair, puffing intermittently on his pipe, but I, who knew him well, could recognise the tell-tale signs of alertness and excitement: the sparkle in his eye, the gently pursed lip and the contracted brow.

'The three years that have passed since the kidnapping of the King,' continued Colonel Sapt, 'have been three sad and painful years for Ruritania. As I hinted earlier, Rudolf was not the material from which great kings are moulded, but it would seem that the ordeal in the castle at Zenda had disturbed and weakened his character further. He was a bad husband to Flavia, neglectful and inconsiderate, and an unreliable and erratic monarch to his people. He would shift from long periods of depression and melancholia to bursts of irrational and often violent behaviour. The result of this was that, despite all efforts to reduce the effects of his unstable conduct and hush up reports of the royal indiscretions, the support and devotion he commanded on his accession, both with the court and the people, dwindled. In this climate of general dissatisfaction with Rudolf there sprang up in the country an underground faction bent on gaining enough support to usurp the throne. They are called the Blues and their insignia is the blue bugle – a flower common in our country and, in fact, across all Europe to Asia. At the head of this group is that fiendish rogue, Rupert of Hentzau.'

'What!' I queried, 'Is he still at liberty?'

'Alas, Doctor, he is. There was no way in which he could be officially charged with treason without the whole story of the King's substitution being revealed, and that would have weakened Rudolf's position even further. Therefore Rupert had to be allowed his freedom, for the King's sake.'

'A dark irony, indeed,' commented Holmes.

'We have, of course, more than once attempted to get rid of this thorn in our flesh, but Rupert is too wily and slippery to be caught in our traps. He seems to have the Devil's own luck, but one day, Mr Holmes, one day . . . '

Sapt's voice sank to hoarse whisper and his eyes blazed angrily for an instant before he resumed his narrative.

'Rupert reappeared in Strelsau on the day of Rudolf's wedding to Flavia. He behaved in public as though nothing had happened and, of course, to all but a few who knew the story of the Zenda plot, nothing had happened. Although Michael was dead, his murder had been blamed on an unknown assassin and his treachery was undisclosed. Rupert knew he had nothing to fear – his knowledge made him a secure man. Shortly after his return he took over the Castle of Zenda, which Michael, in his folly, had bequeathed him. It is from the castle that he now commands the Blues. He has not, not as yet, taken any direct action to harm the King, but his presence is like a dark and ominous threat. He is like a spider secretly spinning his web of intrigue, a web that one day may enmesh us all. We must thank God for Queen Flavia, for it is mainly due to her that the Crown maintains any allegiance and respect in the nation. Despite Rudolf's neglect and callousness, she has stood by him, providing the only spark of real honour left with the monarchy. She has sublimated all feelings for the demands of duty.

'Once a year Fritz von Tarlenheim travels to Dresden, carrying a love token from Flavia to Rudolf Rassendyll, whom he meets there. Under the Queen's strict instructions, Fritz has revealed nothing of her misery and the unhappy situation in Ruritania, but conveys only a brief message confirming her undying love. Rassendyll reciprocates with a similar message and token. In some ways, Mr Holmes, this tenuous contact is the only light in Flavia's heavens. Without it I believe she would succumb to the pressures of her tragic marriage and the increasing vulnerability of her position as Queen.'

'The King has no notion of her feelings towards Rassendyll?' I asked.

Sapt shook his head. 'None. I am sure of it.' The colonel shifted his position in the chair, leaning forward with an almost conspiratorial air. 'Now I come to the events that have occurred within the last two months, the direct result of which is the purpose of my visit to England and, indirectly, the reason for my need to enlist your aid.

'Five weeks ago, the King, after one of his all-night drinking bouts, fell ill. The chill he caught developed into a fever and for several days it seemed as though he would die. His demise, of course, would be a triumph for the Blues, for as yet there is no heir to the throne and with Rudolf's death the Crown would fall to the strongest force – Rupert of Hentzau.

'However, the King did recover. At least, he regained his physical health, but the fever had wrought a great change to his mind. As you will have gathered, Rudolf Elfberg was not the most mentally stable of men at the best of times, but this illness seems to have gnawed away at the weak structures of his mind, until they have collapsed altogether. Mr Holmes, not to put too fine a point on it – the King is mad.'

Even Holmes was taken aback at this revelation. 'Mad? In what sense, Colonel Sapt?'

'Oh, he does not gibber and rant or tear his clothes. It is as though he were a child – a natural.' Sapt shook his head slowly. 'He is a pitiful sight to behold.'

'And this state is permanent?'

'There is no certainty as to what might happen. Discreet consultations have been made with some of the most eminent medical authorities in Europe, including Sir Jasper Meek, the specialist in brain disorders from London. They all say the same: whether the mind struggles back to rationality or whether it sinks further into its own oblivion depends upon the personality of the victim and the fight he is prepared to make for his own sanity. Only time will tell. The King's condition is known to only a few: the Queen, myself, Fritz, Steiner, the King's personal physician, the Chancellor, and a small number of trusted and reliable servants. The story given out publicly is that the King has a spinal injury, the result of his being thrown from his horse, and so all public duties are cancelled until he has fully recovered. The suggestion of recklessness connected with a riding accident has helped give the story a certain credence and so this version of the truth has been readily accepted – for the moment. But it will not be long before the people grow restless, wanting to see their monarch.'

'Does Rupert suspect the truth?' I asked.

'I do not know for certain, Doctor Watson, but one must never underestimate the cunning of the man. If he does not know now, it will only be a matter of time before he discovers the truth. And we are running desperately short of time. In just ten days the King of Bohemia is due to visit our country on a State Visit. If Rudolf is not present to receive him and attend the various public ceremonies connected with the visit, we have no hope of preventing the people from learning the true facts. It would be the final blow. How could they be expected to continue their allegiance to a weak and thought-less king who has now degenerated into madness? And waiting in the wings, ready to snatch their support, is Rupert of Hentzau. Hah! It would be like presenting him with the keys of the kingdom. It is just such an opportunity that he and his devilish crew have been waiting for, to seize power and bring destruction to the Elfberg line. This must be prevented at all costs.'

Holmes jerked forward in his chair, his eyes glinting brightly in the firelight. 'Now it is clear to me why, when your country is on the brink of disaster, you leave it to journey to England. Once more you wish to engage the services of Rudolf Rassendyll to impersonate the King in order to allay the suspicions of the people and confound the machinations of Rupert.'

'You are as shrewd and perceptive as your reputation suggests you are, Mr Holmes. That is precisely why I came to London. Knowing of Rassendyll's love of adventure, his honourable character and his deep feelings for Queen Flavia, I saw no difficulty in persuading him to come to the aid of the Ruritanian monarchy once again.'

'Your presence in my chambers, however, suggests to me that you have encountered some difficulty in your mission.'

'I have, Mr Holmes. Rudolf Rassendyll has disappeared!'

Chapter Four

The missing substitute

Sherlock Holmes sat silent for some moments with his brows knitted and his eyes fixed on the fire. Then, with a sudden movement, he turned to me, his face beaming.

'We seem to have reached familiar territory at last, eh, Watson?'

He rubbed his thin hands and once more addressed our visitor. 'Now, Colonel, let us be precise about this. In what way exactly has Rudolf Rassendyll disappeared?'

'Rassendyll lives in the country, in a little hamlet called Langton Green, near Tunbridge Wells. I made my way down to this rural backwater and sought out his dwelling. It is a modest villa in which, according to Fritz, he lives a secluded life attended by only one servant. This servant, Roberts, a man of some sixty years, told me that his master had gone up to London to spend some time with his brother, Lord Burlesdon. Cursing the wasted journey, I returned to the city and found my way to Lord Burlesdon's address in Park Lane. After some persuasion with various lackeys, I gained an interview with the noble lord, who, to be frank, was most discourteous in his attentions to me. In a rather brusque and off-hand manner, he informed me that he was not his brother's keeper and that he had not seen or communicated with Rudolf for some time, nor did he expect to.

'I cannot tell you why exactly, but I believe he was lying. I have been too long in public life for any man to fool me with blatant falsehoods. He was uneasy and there was no conviction in his voice. He tried to cover his uncertainty with arrogance and lack of interest. Of course, there was nothing I could do but accept his story and leave. There is my dilemma, Mr Holmes. Can you help me?'

Holmes rose and paced the floor for some minutes, pausing at one point to peer behind the blind into the street below. Eventually he came to stand by Sapt, with his back to the fire. 'Can I help you? A leading question, Colonel Sapt. I cannot wave a magic wand and carry out the conjurer's art in reverse to make Rassendyll appear from thin air. However, I can apply my knowledge, brain and experience to the problem which certainly seems to present many unique features. The first task is to assemble more data. Tell me, does Rupert know of your mission?'

'It is highly unlikely. Only the Queen and Fritz know the purpose of my visit. I will be missed at Court, of course, but Rupert can have no idea of my whereabouts. I left the country surreptitiously and alone.'

'I wonder,' mused Holmes slowly and then shook his head. 'If the man is as clever and as cunning as you have led us to believe, then surely he did not need to be told of your plan: he should be capable of following your train of thought. Realising that Rassendyll was your only salvation, he took steps to get to him first.'

'Damnation, Holmes. It's impossible!' roared Sapt.

Holmes gave him a bleak smile. 'Not only is it possible; I fear it is probable. All indications point in that direction. But what about yourself? Have you felt threatened in any way or sensed that you were being watched since your arrival here?'

Sapt shook his head. 'No, not that I know of. At least . . . ' He paused.

'Yes,' snapped Holmes, 'there is something?'

'Well, nothing of any real consequence. It's just a trivial thing.'

'It is my experience that trivial matters are usually of the greatest importance. Please allow me to judge.'

'Well, it is only that, when I visited Lord Burlesdon earlier today, I noticed an odd-looking character loitering across the road and when I left he was still there.'

'Was he a tall man with a checked cap, walrus moustache, and wearing a shabby grey ulster?'

Sapt's eyes widened in astonishment. 'My God, you are a conjurer. How did you know that?'

'Because the very same man is standing across the street from these rooms at this moment,' Holmes replied.

'What!' Sapt shot from his chair, but Holmes swiftly restrained him.

'No, Colonel, don't look. Let's leave him in his ignorance, thinking that we are unaware of his surveillance. That way he may be of use to us.'

Sapt resumed his seat.

'What does this mean, Holmes?' I enquired.

'I think it is quite obvious what it means: our friend here has been followed by Count Rupert's men, probably since he left Ruritania.'

'If that is the case,' said Sapt, 'then they will know the object of my mission and will be prepared to do all in their power to prevent Rassendyll from returning to Strelsau.'

'Under the Elfberg colours, certainly.'

'He would never go under Rupert's.'

'Not willingly, maybe.'

'You mean . . . ?'

'That Rassendyll has been abducted by the Blues. On the evidence we have in our possession at the moment, that seems the most likely conclusion.'

Sapt looked crestfallen. 'But Rassendyll would rather die than submit to Rupert's demands,' he murmured.

'There are more ways than one to force a man to do as you wish. We are still very much in the dark in this affair; we need more light to illuminate this situation.'

'What do you suggest we do?'

'I believe we should enlist the aid of our acquaintance across the street.'

'How?'

Holmes paused before replying. 'You are staying at the Charing Cross Hotel, are you not?'

'I am, but how did you know that?'

'It is not important.'

'Maybe not to you, but I should like to know.'

'Very well. It was a simple deduction. The Charing Cross is a popular hotel with visiting Europeans and at present there are some road works by the Villiers Street entrance which have caused the surrounding pavement to become coated with a layer of reddish clay peculiar to the district. A fair quantity of this is adhering to the heels of both your boots.'

Sapt gave a barking laugh. 'Obviously I have come to the right man to solve my problems,' he averred.

Holmes's features remained stern. 'We shall see. Now, Colonel, I suggest you return to your hotel. No doubt that, as you do so, your follower will hail a cab and pursue you. Call out your destination clearly and, once aboard, give whispered instructions to your cabby to take the journey at a leisurely pace.'

'Why?'

'Because while you are being followed by "Checked Cap", Watson and I shall be on his tail.' Holmes turned to me. 'You are agreeable, Watson?'

'Certainly,' said I.

'Good, then I see no reason for delay. Once you arrive at your hotel, Colonel, linger a while in the lobby until you see Watson and me arrive, then retire to your room for the night. We shall contact you in the morning and give you a progress report.'

The bulky Ruritanian stood up. 'Mr Holmes, I can't thank you enough.'

'You are premature in your gratitude. As yet, nothing has been achieved.'

'That may be so, but you have given me hope that all is not lost.'

'These are dark waters, Colonel, and I suspect that we haven't touched bottom yet.'

*   *   *

Minutes later, Holmes, stationed at the window, observed Sapt leave by our front door and board the cab he had kept waiting for him. The spy across the street, who had been lounging under a gas lamp, waited until the horse began to pull away from the kerb before he galvanised himself into action. Throwing his cigarette away, he darted into the road and hailed a cab.

'Come, Watson,' hissed Holmes.

With all speed we left our chambers, dashed down the stairs and were on the pavement in time to see 'Checked Cap' board his cab, which then followed Sapt's down Baker Street. Holmes spied a third cab and sprang forward to engage it. The vehicle came to a halt, but the driver looked down at us and shook his head.

'Sorry, gents, but I can't oblige you. I have to get back to the stables in Crawford Street.'

'An extra half sovereign at the end of our journey, if you'll take us,' offered my friend.

The man hesitated momentarily, but still shook his head. 'I'd like to, guv'nor, but me horse has gorn and lost a shoe and she needs attention quick.'

Holmes gave an exasperated gasp and turned on his heel. 'This way, Watson,' he snapped, setting off down Baker Street in the direction taken by the two hansoms.

Luckily Sapt had followed Holmes's instructions and his cab was making but slow progress: consequently we were able to keep both vehicles in view as we sprinted after them. While we ran, I frantically looked around for another cab, but there was none in sight. The cold wind whipped our faces, its icy sting causing my eyes to water.

'Of all the infernal luck!' panted Holmes, his words caught by the breeze and swept away.

Imperceptibly the distance between us and the nearer cab lengthened.

'We must not lose him,' Holmes gasped, again putting on an extra burst of speed, leaving me several yards behind.

As we neared Oxford Street, the pavements grew busier, further hindering our progress as we dodged in and out of the oncoming flow of pedestrians. At one point I collided with a stocky fellow of rough appearance who was most put out by the encounter. He made a grab for me, but I did not stop and, dodging his clutches, made my apologies to him over my shoulder.

Approaching the corner of Hardinge Street we spied a waiting cab. Holmes vaulted aboard, gave hurried instructions to the driver and then turned to pull me inside. I was jerked breathless into my seat as the vehicle leapt into motion.

'Nothing like a little exercise to put colour in the cheeks and a spring in the step, eh, Watson?' remarked Holmes with a dry chuckle, his keen face exultant in the dim light of the cab.

We turned left into Oxford Street, following the spy's cab. Despite the lateness of the hour and unpleasant weather conditions, the thoroughfare was thronged with people: theatre-goers homeward bound, late night revellers in evening dress, shift workers and the various miscellaneous flotsam and jetsam that float through the great city at all hours. There were ill-assorted groups of itinerants, huddled in doorways, engaged in animated conversations.

'The human animal is a gregarious beast by compulsion. It must be out and mixing with its own kind,' commented Holmes, without taking his eyes off the cab some hundred yards ahead of us.

Then a strange thing occurred. Instead of turning right at Oxford Circus and down Regent Street in the wake of Sapt's cab, the spy's hansom continued straight ahead.

'Right,' Holmes exclaimed excitedly, 'Watson, you're on your own. Follow Sapt back to his hotel and wait for me in the lobby. I must keep on the trail of this cove. The fact that he's not following Sapt may mean he feels he is safe for tonight and he can pick up the trail in the morning. Or it may mean that his spell of duty is over and he's handed over to another tail. Whatever the reason, if I keep after him, he may lead me to Rassendyll.'

Our cab had slowed to a crawl as it negotiated Oxford Circus, allowing me to jump down without difficulty.

'Take care, Holmes,' I called as I landed on the pavement at the far side of the circus. He gave me a brief wave in reply. Before turning to pick up Sapt's trail, I watched Holmes's cab for a few moments before it was swallowed up by the night.

Chapter Five
The Charing Cross Hotel

I crossed Oxford Street and hurried into Regent Street. It was only seconds before I was able to engage a cab in which to follow Colonel Sapt back to the Charing Cross Hotel.

I sat in the dark recess of the cab with the thrill of adventure once more in my heart and let my mind wander over the details of the strange affair in which Holmes and I had become involved. I gave a wry smile as I remembered how, earlier in the evening, I had been attempting, not very successfully, to coax Holmes out of his melancholia with trifling tests of deduction and now, but a few hours later, each of us was travelling across London following separate threads of a highly important and dangerous mystery.

As my cab neared Piccadilly Circus Sapt's hansom was in clear view ahead of me, and so it remained for the ten minutes before we arrived at our destination. The Charing Cross Hotel is a large, impressive, French Renaissance-styled edifice facing on to the Strand, an integral part of the great railway station, one of London's gateways to the continent. My cab pulled up just in time for me to see Sapt pay off his driver and pass through the portals of the hotel. Seconds later I did likewise.

It was now nearing midnight, but the lobby was crowded and noisy. A throng of people paraded through in various directions. Some were checking in, while others were on their way out, obviously with the intention of sampling some of the more dubious pleasures to be obtained in the city at this late hour. Some guests were lounging quietly in comfortable armchairs reading, enjoying a nightcap or the last smoke of the day.

In among the crush and hubbub, I soon espied Sapt. He had retrieved one of the evening papers from the desk and had seated himself in a prominent position near the lift. I could tell that the contents of the paper held no interest for him; it was a mere property to use while he furtively surveyed the room. At length his gaze fell on me and our eyes exchanged signs of recognition. I saw by his expression that he was puzzled by the absence of Holmes, his eyes searching the room in vain and then returning to me. I tried to give him assurance that all was well by appearing to be completely at ease. He seemed to sense my meaning and, after a while, when the human traffic in the lobby had diminished, Sapt discarded the newspaper, performed some exaggerated yawning actions for my benefit to indicate that he was retiring for the night, obtained his key from the reception desk and made his way to the lift. On entering he gave me a brief nod of acknowledgement before the lift door closed.

There was nothing for me to do now but sit tight and await the arrival of Sherlock Holmes. I knew that I might have a long wait on my hands as there was no way of telling where the spy's trail had led him or in what exploits he had become involved. I realised the futility of surmise, so I attempted, to the best of my ability, to push some contemplations out of my mind.

It was shortly after two in the morning when my friend finally put in an appearance. By that time the lobby was almost deserted, apart from a few nodding guests and the night staff. I had moved to one of the armchairs by then and was examining the pages of an evening paper for the hundredth time when Holmes strode into the hotel. His face was flushed and his eyes were eager with excitement. I assumed that his adventures had met with a degree of success.

He pulled up a chair to mine. 'All goes well, I trust?' said he in a whisper.

I nodded. 'I have encountered no problems. But what about you? Where did "Checked Cap" lead you? Are we any nearer solving the mystery? Do you know where Rassendyll is?'

His reply was offhand and accompanied by a dismissive gesture. 'There will be time for such details later,' he said and turned to survey the room.

It was one of Holmes's most annoying traits that he would keep vital information to himself until it suited him to reveal it, usually at a moment when he could create the most dramatic effect. It was very frustrating, often causing me to take action without knowing the reason. However, I knew from past experience that there was no point in challenging him on this issue. If he wanted to be a clam, there was no prising him open.

He turned back to me. 'Sapt has gone to his room?'

I acknowledged this was so.

'No sign of surveillance,' he frowned.

'Did you expect any?'

'I'm not sure,' he replied in a somewhat preoccupied manner.

After a moment's thought, he spoke again. 'Well, Watson, I'm afraid we will have to disturb the Colonel's slumbers. I have a most important question to ask him concerning a young boy.'

'A boy?'

Holmes made no reply.

Sapt had told us back at our Baker Street rooms that he was occupying a small suite on the third floor, to where Holmes and I now headed. We took the lift up and shortly found ourselves in a dimly lit corridor outside Sapt's room. Holmes tapped lightly on the door. We waited some moments, but there was no reply.

'Deep in the arms of Morpheus,' I suggested.

Holmes tapped louder.

'He must be a heavy sleeper if that did not rouse him,' he remarked.

'What now?'

'There is nothing for it, but to effect an entry.' So saying, he produced a small length of wire from his waistcoat pocket and applied it to the keyhole. Holmes had mentioned more than once in the past that, had he not turned his attentions to the detection of crime, he would have made an expert burglar. Here was proof indeed, for within seconds there was a decisive click and Holmes turned the handle and opened the door.

We entered the darkened room. Pale moonlight filtered in through a window at the far end, but it was only sufficient for us to gauge a rough geography of the chamber.

I saw the gleam of an electric light switch and motioned to use it, but Holmes restrained me. From the folds of his ulster he extracted his pocket lantern and lit it. He flashed the beam around, revealing a small, but elegant, sitting room. The light finally came to rest on a door at the far corner.

'The bedroom,' I whispered. 'That's why Sapt did not hear your knock.'

Without comment Holmes made swiftly and silently for the door. As we entered I was immediately aware of the smell of cigar smoke. The curtains were drawn and the room was in total darkness save for the searching yellow finger of Holmes's lantern. Eventually the beam fell on the bed. There lay Sapt, his head protruding from the covers.

However, the expression his face wore chilled me to the marrow. His eyes were wide open in a startled, fixed stare and his mouth gaped in what appeared to be a silent scream.

Holmes rushed to the bedside, briefly touching Sapt's forehead, before pulling the covers back to show the Colonel fully dressed in the clothes he had worn in our company earlier that evening. But what arrested the attention and made me gasp out loud was that protruding from his chest was the hilt of an ornate dagger around which a dark crimson stain was spreading outwards.

'Murdered,' I croaked in a hoarse, horrified whisper.

Holmes gave a stern nod and, with a sigh of dismay, swung the beam of the lantern around the room, finally bringing it back to rest on the inert body. It was only then that I noticed a small object lying in the centre of Sapt's open palm.

It was a single, small flower.

'The blue bugle,' said Holmes solemnly.

We stood with bitter hearts, momentarily overwhelmed by this sudden and devastating blow to our investigations.

'They have been too clever and too quick for us,' Holmes muttered, his face darkening with anger as he gazed at the blood-stained corpse of Colonel Sapt. 'I should have ensured that he was under close surveillance at all times.'

I knew that he was directing his fury as much against himself for what he regarded as his shortcomings as he was against our protagonists.

'There was no way that you could have foreseen this tragic outcome,' I assured him.

Holmes shook his head and heaved a heavy sigh. 'I know you mean well, old friend, but you are wrong. I should have prevented this.'

Before I had a chance to reply, he handed me his pocket lantern. 'Hold this for me, will you, while I make a brief examination of the room.'

While I directed the beam on his instructions, Holmes ranged around the bedroom, inspecting various parts with his lens. So swiftly was it carried out that one would hardly have guessed the minuteness with which it was conducted.

'There is little to learn here, except that our murderer was certainly a cool customer,' he said at last, holding up a small ashtray. 'It seems that he enjoyed a smoke after his callous crime.' He sighed once more. 'Well, Watson, the first round is to Rupert and his crew, but the battle is far from over. Are you game for further adventures tonight?'

'Of course.'

'Good man. Are you armed?'

I produced my pistol in reply.

'Keep it to hand,' he instructed. 'You may need it before the night is over.'

Chapter Six

A London dawn

The clear lugubrious tones of Big Ben striking three o'clock rang out over the sleeping city. The wind had now dropped and the night air was still. Holmes and I were once more ensconced in a hansom cab traversing the silent streets of London. It was some time after our speedy and discreet departure from the Charing Cross Hotel. We had left Sapt's room undisturbed as we had found it.

'To raise the alarm would only delay us and seriously hamper our investigations,' Holmes had explained. 'There is nothing we can do for the Colonel now. Nothing but avenge his murder and complete the task he left in our hands.'

As our cab moved through the empty streets, dimly illuminated by flaring gas lamps and moonlight appearing from a cloudy sky, it felt, to my tired brain, as though we were riding into a dream land-scape. The dark profiles of familiar buildings, the hushed thoroughfares and the eerie staccato tread of the horse lent an air of unreality to the journey.

'Are you all right, Watson,' asked my friend sharply.

'Yes,' I replied, shaking off my seductive imaginings. 'But tell me, Holmes, where are we heading?'

'Forgive me, Watson, I should have told you earlier. It was not my intention to keep you in the dark. I was simply preoccupied with my own thoughts. We are now retracing my journey of earlier this evening. After leaving you at Oxford Circus, my cab kept on the trail of "Checked Cap". We travelled east towards Stepney and on to the Mile End Road. Just before it turns into Bow Road we turned right into Burdett Road. Some three hundred yards down there, our friend came to rest.'

Holmes gave a dry chuckle. ' "Checked cap" was oblivious of my presence. So relaxed and confident was he that he gave a cheery "good-night" to the cabby. He then entered a modest detached villa, number 104. The curtains were drawn in the downstairs window bay, but I was able to observe chinks of bright light through the odd gap, indicating that there were others in the house: others involved in the conspiracy.

'On further investigation I discovered a small lane running behind the row of houses. Going down there I was able to clamber over a wall into the back yard of number 104. The garden was neglected and overgrown, and the rear of the house was in darkness. I could not, of course, light my lantern, for fear of being detected. I was just about to make my way round the side when, as luck would have it, I saw a glimmer of light at my feet. It was then that I could see a grating covered with weeds and grasses situated just above a small cellar window.

'My vision was hampered by the foliage and the grime on the pane, but what I did see set my heart racing. There in the cellar was a woman holding a candlestick, the source of the illumination. She seemed to be inspecting something on the floor. As she moved round, shedding more light in my direction, I was able to observe that the object of her interest was the body of a young boy. He was lying on a makeshift bed of rough sacking. At first I thought the boy was dead, but then he stirred in his slumbers. After inspecting the boy for some moments, the woman left, plunging the room into darkness once more.'

'Who on earth is the boy?'

'I have my suspicions, but until I have more data, I'd rather not air them.'

'You were hoping that Sapt might tell you.'

'Not exactly, but he could have confirmed what I suspect.'

'What did you do next?'

'I crept round to the front of the house and peered through one of the gaps in the drawn curtains. My viewpoint was limited, but I could see it was a shabbily furnished room. "Checked Cap" was there, sprawled on a *chaise longue*, swilling down some gin and conversing with another man whose face I could not see, although he did appear to be wearing some kind of light blue uniform. The woman I had seen in the cellar joined them and they chatted amicably for some time. I could not hear what they said, but I did catch two names which they mentioned more than once. One was Sapt.'

'And the other?'

'Holstein.'

I shook my head. 'That means nothing to me.'

'Nor to me, at present. It is a name to store away. After a while the trio made as if to retire for the night. From what I could gather, "Checked Cap" had some claim on the woman. Just before leaving the room, he came to the window. I threw myself to the ground and pressed against the wall, as he pulled back the curtain to scan the street. He was, I assume, checking that all was well before retiring. Luckily I had managed to get out of sight before he spotted me. Shortly after, the door was bolted and the light extinguished. I realised that I had gleaned as much as I was able to for the time being, so I made my way back to the Hotel.'

'What does it all mean?'

'Putting aside the presence of the boy in the cellar for the moment, it seems that the house is being used as the headquarters of the Blues while they are in London. As I suspected, they have followed Sapt from Ruritania, establishing themselves in rented property here while they set about capturing Rassendyll and murdering Sapt. How much less suspicious if the King's confidant is killed away from Strelsau, thus allowing no trace of blame to be attached to Rupert and his cohorts.'

'And what of Rassendyll? Do you think they have hidden him in the house?'

'I firmly believe the Blues have him in their clutches, but, if my deductions are correct, he is not in the house, but at this minute on his way back to the continent with Sapt's assassin.'

'From what we have been told of Rassendyll, he would rather die than yield to their demands. How could he be made to go?'

'The boy is the bait.'

My face must have betrayed my puzzlement at his reply, for Holmes gave me a thin smile and patted my arm. 'I will explain all in due course, but now, Watson, we are nearing our destination.'

So engrossed had I been in Holmes's narrative that I had not noticed how the scenery had changed from the tall noble edifices of the City of London to the shabbier, ramshackle properties of the East End. At Holmes's command the cab turned into Burdett Road.

I was still unsure what Holmes's plan of action involved. Would he suggest we burst into the house on our own and attempt to capture the residents?

A short way down the road Holmes gave the cabby instructions to pull in and wait for us. Quietly, we moved down the deserted road until we came upon number 104, a dark irregular silhouette against the paler moonwashed sky.

'Now, Watson,' said Holmes in hushed tones, 'I will stand guard here. I want to be sure that none of these birds fly the coop until you return with reinforcements. Unless my memory fails me, our old friend Gregson is on late duty at the Yard this month. Tell him we need his services and those of about half a dozen able-bodied men. Off you go now. Any delay jeopardises the success of this venture.'

*   *   *

The pale grey light of dawn was seeping across the sky when I once more approached Burdett Road. Now I was accompanied by Inspector Tobias Gregson of Scotland Yard, who, with the efficiency and professionalism that had moved Holmes to call him 'the smartest of the Scotland Yarders', had acted with commendable alacrity. Following behind our cab was a police vehicle disguised as a trader's wagon and containing six constables.

We stopped some distance up the road from number 104. Gregson instructed his men to remain silent and out of sight while he consulted Holmes, whose spare figure we espied still on guard by the gateway.

'Glad you could make it, Gregson,' my friend said warmly as the two shook hands.

'I must admit, Mr Holmes, I've never known you to raise a false alarm in the past, but I do hope that you have a good reason for this little excursion.' The tall, flaxen-haired policeman inclined his head in the direction of the police wagon.

'I have indeed, Gregson. There will be time for full details later, but suffice it to say that the occupants of the house are foreign anarchists, who have already been responsible for the murder of a visiting dignitary from the Ruritanian Court.'

The official detective's pale face relaxed briefly into a knowing grin. 'Very well, Mr Holmes. What's your plan of action?'

'Station your men at the front and rear of the house to stop anyone escaping, while Watson, you and I force an entry. They have a lad captive in the cellar and it is him above all we must protect.'

Gregson was familiar enough with my friend's methods to act on his instructions without further question. Some minutes later, with dawn now lifting the dark veil of night from the dingy road, we were ready to move.

'The front door is bolted, so we'll have to make a rather clumsy entrance through the window,' said Holmes, picking up a large stone from the garden. He hurled it at the side bay window, which shattered on impact. Breaking the jagged glass shards still protruding from the frame with the butts of our pistols, we clambered into the darkened house.

Already the noise of our entry had alerted the inhabitants. Muffled cries and hurried movements could be heard from upstairs. With Holmes leading the way we rushed from the sitting room into the hallway and, as we reached the bottom of the stairs, a figure appeared on the landing. Yellow sparks flew from his raised hand, followed by the sound of a shot. I felt a bullet whizz past my head and ricochet off the wall behind me.

Holmes returned fire. The figure gave a sharp cry of pain and clutched its right shoulder before retreating into the shadows. Slowly we mounted the stairs, Holmes stopping us with a raised hand as we reached the landing. Although the morning light was struggling into the house, the head of the stairs was bathed in gloom.

Suddenly there was a noise to our right and then another shot rang out. Gregson gave a gasp, dropped to his knees and slumped against the wall. As we turned our attention to him, out of nowhere it seemed came the figure of a frenzied woman. With a scream of fury she launched herself on Holmes. Such was the surprise and ferocity of her attack that he had no chance to protect himself and, in the ensuing struggle, his gun was knocked from his grasp to the floor.

I was momentarily mesmerised by the attack of this she-devil. Her fingers, like the vicious talons of some giant bird, clawed at Holmes's face, straining to rip and tear. By grasping her wrists, he managed to hold them at bay, but, as he struggled with her, they both fell against the bannister rail, which emitted an ominous groan at the impact. I was shaken from my temporary paralysis by the sound of another shot ringing out. I glimpsed 'Checked Cap' dodging from one room to another down the corridor to our right. I aimed at the fleeting figure, but he merged with the darkness before I could fire.

Holmes was still grappling with the woman. She was like a creature possessed, with her claws slicing the air, the sharp nails slashing perilously close to Holmes's eyes. Already there was a dark trail of blood down his right cheek. As they fought, she shrieked, spitting out a series of black oaths. Once more they crashed against the bannister which bellied outwards with their weight and then, with a sequence of complaining groans, it swayed, splintered, cracked and, in an explosion of sawdust, gave way. Both bodies teetered on the brink, almost motionless for a time it seemed, before they began their plunge to the hall below.

I leaped forward and grabbed for Holmes. My fingers clutching a handful of his coat, I pulled violently, jerking him backward on to the landing before his feet lost their grip. However, the woman, who in terror had relinquished her hold of Holmes, was now grasping frantically at the air, her arms flailing in wild desperation. She gave a terrified scream and toppled over the edge, her body plummeting downwards, making nightmarish swimming motions before it crashed to the ground.

'Thank you, Watson,' said Holmes, a little breathless as he steadied himself. After retrieving his gun he turned his attention to the slumped figure of the Scotland Yard man. Gregson was conscious and clutching his knee, a trickle of blood running through his fingers. Crouching on the top step I examined his wound.

'Don't bother about me now, Watson,' he ground out. 'I'll live.'

'Can you move?' I asked.

'Only with some difficulty,' he grimaced, shifting his position slightly.

Holmes knelt beside me.

'It's better if we leave you here, Gregson, until we've dealt with our other two friends.'

'Of course. I've got my gun. I can act as sentry. No one will get past me.'

Before any more could be said our attention was arrested by a sudden sound behind us. As I turned I saw two dark shapes about to launch themselves at us. 'Checked Cap' let fly with his boot at the kneeling figure of Holmes, but he, with great dexterity, dodged sideways and clamped his fingers on the assailant's foot. With a sharp twist and tug, Holmes sent his attacker flying past him, head first down the staircase.

Meanwhile, Gregson, lying pinned against the wall, had used his gun on the other fellow, who had staggered back, clutching his breast, before falling to the floor – dead.

'Checked Cap' quickly recovered from his fall and was in retreat.

'He mustn't get to the boy,' Holmes cried, vaulting down the stairs. I followed in pursuit.

On reaching the cellar door, 'Checked Cap' turned and fired wildly in our direction, stopping us in our tracks, as we flung ourselves against the wall to avoid the ricocheting bullets.

This delay gave our adversary time enough to fling himself into the cellar and slam the door shut. Holmes, with electric speed, launched himself at the door before it could be bolted on the inside.

Such was the force of his action that the door burst open, crashing into 'Checked Cap' on the other side. The vigour of the blow was sufficient to knock him off balance, causing him to stagger backwards down the cellar steps. Only by grasping the handrail for support was he able to keep an upright position.

On reaching the bottom, he steadied himself and gazed around the gloomy room before aiming his pistol. But his target was not Holmes or me, his pursuers, but the dim shape huddled on rough sacking at the far side of the cellar. There was a sharp blaze from Holmes's revolver and 'Checked Cap' staggered, his glance falling on us, before his eyeballs rolled upwards and he crumpled on to the stone flagging.

When we reached him I saw in the dim grey light that he had breathed his last. 'Well, at least Sapt has been avenged,' I said softly.

Holmes made no comment, but raced across to inspect the inert figure of the boy. Kneeling by him, my friend turned the youth's face sideways: the features were smooth and pale, except for the dark blemish of a bruise on the right cheek. The eyelids fluttered erratically, but remained closed.

'Drugged, would you say, Watson?'

I took the boy's pulse and, lifting back the lids, examined the pupils. 'Yes,' I said. 'He's very heavily sedated, but nothing worse than that.'

'Thank heavens.' Holmes looked over to the corpse at the foot of the stairs. 'Quite a bloodbath,' he commented quietly, as though speaking to himself. He was silent for a moment and then he turned to me, his face drawn and worried. 'We may have saved the boy and avenged Sapt, Watson, but we have left ourselves without any prisoners who could have provided us with vital information to aid our quest. Now we are left to unravel the next thread in this convoluted affair on our own.'

Chapter Seven
A family reunion

Life was never dull, sharing it as I did with the foremost consulting detective of our time, but when Holmes and I were on a case I seemed to undergo a heightening of my senses, so much so that I felt sometimes as though I was propelled into a different dimension. It had a dream-like quality to it, and yet all apprehensions were crystal clear, the nerves were keener and the brain functioned at a faster rate. I find it strange to relate that I have never previously made reference to this sensation when recording the many other adventures my friend and I shared, but I believe that it has in no small measure affected my telling of them. It is this element in his chronicles, the romantic ambience, as he regarded it, that made Holmes deride and condemn my literary efforts.

On one occasion he was scathing in his criticism. 'You have degraded what should have been a course of lectures into a series of tales. You have erred, perhaps, in attempting to put colour and life into each of your statements, instead of confining yourself to the task of placing on record that severe reasoning from cause to effect which is really the only notable feature about the thing.'

The 'severe reasoning', his *raison d'etre*, was so highly tuned that he sometimes failed to note the dramatic consequences of his investigations. I was not guilty of putting 'colour and life' into them; they were there already. Sherlock Holmes was a cerebral animal, and it was his mind that was stimulated by his investigations. He did not sense the quickening of life as I did once the game was afoot – and never did I experience it with greater intensity than in the Hentzau affair. After that stormy cab ride to the Charing Cross Hotel, one startling event seemed to tumble after another. Recalling the case, as I do now in sober and tranquil mood, I can still re-live something of that pulse-quickening excitement and heady whirl of danger I then felt.

Several hours after our dramatic adventure in the East End, Holmes and I were back once more in the familiar surroundings of our Baker

Street apartment. Inspector Gregson had been taken for treatment to the police hospital, while three corpses had been carried to the mortuary at Scotland Yard. The boy had been brought back to Baker Street with us. Holmes had prevailed upon Gregson to let the boy remain in our custody for the time being and the official detective had been too weary to raise any objection. The youth, still in a drugged stupor, was placed in the tender care of our housekeeper, Mrs Hudson, who made up a bed for him in her downstairs parlour.

Since arriving back at our quarters I had tried to rest a little to recoup after the exertions of our exploits and the loss of a night's sleep, but Holmes showed no signs of fatigue. He had plunged himself with alacrity into a series of tasks: he carried out with his microscope and lens a close examination of some of the boy's outer clothing and items gleaned from Sapt's bedroom, sent off a couple of telegrams, consulted *Burke's Peerage* and the *Thomas Cook Continental Timetable*, emitting satisfied grunts as he did so, and pored over a map of central Europe. I knew his mind was too involved with his own thoughts for me to bother him with questions regarding several points that still mystified me.

It was only at ten o'clock, after consuming a hearty breakfast, that he flung himself into his chair by the fire and lit his pipe.

'If all goes well,' he said, stretching his long legs out in front of the fire, 'one or two inconclusive aspects of this affair should be cleared up satisfactorily by noon. Until then, a quiet pipe and a few minutes of repose.'

Without another word he leaned back, the old briar between his lips, his eyes fixed meditatively upon the corner of the ceiling, the blue smoke curling up from him. Silent and motionless, he sat with the morning light shining on his firm-set, aquiline features. So he remained as I drifted into sleep, only to be aroused by a soft knock at the door and the appearance of our landlady.

'The young lad's stirring, Mr Holmes. Perhaps you and Doctor Watson had better attend on him.'

We accompanied Mrs Hudson down to her cosy parlour where the youth was lying on a sofa, covered with several blankets. He was a good looking boy of some ten years with strong features and a rich crop of chestnut hair. He was in the early process of dragging himself from his drug-induced slumbers. The puckered eyelids flickered erratically as he struggled for consciousness.

'This is your department, Watson,' said Holmes, standing aside to allow me to examine the boy.

'His pulse is strengthening,' I was able to say presently. 'If he could be made to take some *café noir* that would speed up the process.'

'Oh, I'll see to that, Doctor,' said Mrs Hudson. 'It's quite a while since I had a wee charge to look after.'

Holmes gave a broad grin. 'We must add ministering angel to all your other sterling qualities. I think, Watson, we can leave the nursing in Mrs Hudson's capable hands. In fact, I suspect we may be in the way.'

Mrs Hudson gave Holmes one of her looks: a mixture of amusement and indignation. She had the greatest respect and affection for her bohemian tenant, but that did not prevent her, on occasion, from airing her disapproval.

'Off with you both,' she said, shooing us from the room.

'As you know, I am not an admirer of womankind in general,' admitted Holmes when we had returned to our fireside, 'but Mrs Hudson is the exception to prove my rule. She is, without doubt, a female paragon.'

Before I was able to agree with this sentiment, there was a disturbance on the stairs outside our room, followed by the door being dashed open. Framed in the opening was a tall, well-built man, dressed formally in a frock coat and carrying a top hat. He took a step into the room, looking from one to the other of us, before resting his tormented gaze on my companion.

'Where is he?' bellowed the intruder. Advancing further into the room, he repeated his question with growing fury.

Holmes rose to his feet and, before our visitor could react, grabbed his arm and led him to a chair by the fire. Our visitor's face, broad and handsome, but bearing the marks of sleepless nights and worry, clouded with confusion, the fire of anger dying in his bloodshot eyes to be replaced by disturbing anxiety. As he sat down, he fumbled inside his coat and produced a crumpled telegram which he waved at my friend.

'What is the meaning of this?' he shouted, but by this time his voice had lost its bombast and was shaking in desperation.

Holmes took the telegram and tossed the message across to me. It read, 'NICHOLAS IS SAFE. SHERLOCK HOLMES, 221B BAKER STREET.'

'I can assure you, Lord Burlesdon, the telegram is no hoax; your son is perfectly safe and will be restored to you presently.'

Burlesdon slumped back in the chair with a sob. 'Thank God,' he uttered. 'Thank God.'

'Watson, I think his Lordship could do with a brandy.'

I quickly administered the restorative to our visitor, who clutched the glass with eager thanks and downed the amber liquid in a single gulp. 'I must apologise,' said he at length, 'for my somewhat unseemly behaviour, but both my wife and I have been under the most intolerable strain since this whole wretched business began.'

'I quite understand,' said Holmes, 'and I do assure you that your son Nicholas is safe, unharmed save for a few bruises, and is at present recovering from a drugged sleep.'

The haggard face of Lord Burlesdon creased with mixed emotions. His eyes brimmed with tears while his mouth split in a broad grin. 'I do not know how to thank you.'

'By answering a few questions and clarifying some points,' replied Holmes starkly, once more assuming the mantle of the detached reasoner.

'Of course,' answered Lord Burlesdon.

'I have the overall picture of events concerning your son's abduction. If I recount the facts to you as I see them, would you be so good as to correct any misconceptions and supply any missing details . . . ?'

Our visitor nodded.

Holmes leaned back in his chair and steepled his fingers. 'Several days ago your son went missing. Later you were informed that he had been abducted. A representative of the kidnappers came to you requesting an interview with your brother, Rudolf Rassendyll, who was in town visiting you. It was his co-operation that the kidnappers required in order for your son to be returned safely. Rassendyll, of course, agreed, no doubt reluctantly, to their demands and left with the kidnapper. You were told that your son would be released after Rassendyll had carried out his task, but until then you were to remain silent regarding both your brother's whereabouts and your son's plight, otherwise you would see neither again.'

Lord Burlesdon's jaw had dropped in amazement. 'That is absolutely correct, Mr Holmes, but how on earth do you know?'

'Through a series of deductions and observations based on data already in my possession, but that is irrelevant. What, if any, detail can you add to the facts I have already presented?'

'Very little. It all happened as you outlined in your account. We were visited by an agent of the kidnappers . . . '

'Description?'

'A tall man, over six feet, with a stiff, military bearing. He wore a large brimmed hat which was pulled well down over his face, so I am unable to give an accurate account of his features. To tell you the truth my mind was too distracted with worry over Nicholas for me to take much notice. He had a full, black beard – which may have been false, for all I know.' He paused, contracting his brows, attempting to dredge further items from the recesses of his mind for Holmes's benefit. 'Oh, yes, there was one thing,' he said at length. 'Naturally the fellow gave no name, but he smoked his own small cheroots and I noticed the initials "H. H." on his case.'

Holmes nodded in satisfaction.

Burlesdon continued. 'As you stated, this man spent some time in a private interview with Rudolf alone. My brother agreed to depart with him in order to ensure the safety of my son. That was two days ago. Since then I have heard nothing.'

'You have no idea who the kidnappers were or what demands they made on your brother?'

Lord Burlesdon shook his head. 'No, I know nothing. All this has seemed like a dreadful nightmare.'

I could see from the twinkle in my friend's eye that he was pleased with Lord Burlesdon's ignorance concerning the Ruritanian connection.

'Did anyone visit you who wished to contact your brother,' I asked guilelessly.

Burlesdon turned towards me. 'Why, yes, strangely enough there was. A Ruritanian acquaintance of his, I gathered, but I had to send him away. I could not disclose the truth.'

Holmes stood up. 'I must thank you, sir, for your honesty and help in confirming my conclusions. Unfortunately, I am unable to do the same for you. The whereabouts of your brother and the various machinations behind the kidnap plot must, for the moment, remain a secret. I cannot at this juncture divulge any more information than I already hold. Your brother's life is still in grave danger and it is imperative for his safety that you remain silent with regard to all aspects of this affair if I am to have any chance at all to save his life.'

For a moment our visitor looked hesitantly at Holmes and then inclined his head in agreement. 'Very well, Mr Holmes, I will do as you ask, but I beg you to contact me as soon as you have any news of Rudolf.'

'You can be assured of that. Now, I think it is time that we restored your son to you.'

When we entered Mrs Hudson's parlour the young lad was sitting up, sipping coffee from a mug. On seeing his father, he let out a cry of joy.

It was a touching reunion. Tears were shed by both father and son and it is true to say that Mrs Hudson and I did not remain unmoved by the scene. Sherlock Holmes, who always found emotions of any kind a hindrance to clear thinking, made an early retreat to our sitting room, leaving the final goodbyes and reassurances to me.

When I returned upstairs, I discovered Holmes staring thoughtfully into the fire.

'All's well that ends well,' said I, breaking into his reverie.

'For father and son. But I regret, my dear Watson, our part in this royal drama is far from over.'

'Tell me,' I demanded, sitting across from my friend, 'have you known all along that the boy was Burlesdon's son and Rassendyll's nephew?'

'It seemed a logical hypothesis. From what Sapt told us of Rudolf Rassendyll, it was clear that no physical force could make him agree to aid Rupert in his plans. He would rather die than play a part, however unwillingly, in the downfall of the Elfberg monarchy. The threat to Queen Flavia's life implicit in such an outcome would be a further spur to Rassendyll's resistance. Therefore more subtle and devious means had to be employed to ensure his assistance. When I discovered the presence of a boy held captive at the house in Burdett Road things slotted into place. I have a passing knowledge of *Burke's Peerage* and I recalled that Lord Burlesdon had one offspring, a lad of similar years. I checked the facts and the boy's name this morning before sending a telegram to the father.

'Rassendyll has no immediate family, so his brother's son became the pawn in this desperate game to force Rassendyll to act for the Blues. You recall Sapt saying that he believed Lord Burlesdon was lying when he denied knowing the whereabouts of his brother. Obviously there was some pressing reason for his behaviour. The abduction of his son, the boy in the cellar, was the cause.'

'So Rassendyll was forced to go with Rupert's man in order to save the life of his nephew?'

'Exactly. And now doubtless he is firmly in Rupert of Hentzau's clutches.'

'In Ruritania?'

'I am afraid so. The fact that his nephew is safe will be of no use to him now.'

'Then all is lost.'

'Oh, no, Watson. Never say that. Although they have gained two days' advantage over us, I do not think Count Rupert will attempt to bring about his coup until the State Visit of the King of Bohemia, so we have some little time at our disposal – that is, if you are game to accompany me to Ruritania.'

'I mean to see this affair to the end.'

'Good man. There is a train leaving for the continent at 5.15 this evening. We must be on it.'

My mind reeled. I had been aware that, logically, the next stage of our investigations would lead us in pursuit of Rassendyll, but the actual prospect of this gave me great apprehension. Although I had the highest regard for the resourcefulness, courage and abilities of my friend, yet I could not help harbouring grave doubts about the eventual success of our mission. I wondered how two Englishmen with no official powers or assistance could challenge a fanatical revolutionary force and prevent the substitution of the monarch. I realised this must be Sherlock Holmes's greatest challenge and I had doubts if he could meet it.

My musings were interrupted by the arrival of a telegram brought in by Mrs Hudson. Holmes received it as though he had been expecting it. He ripped it open and murmured in satisfaction.

'Spruce yourself up, Watson,' he said, consulting his pocket watch. 'We have a luncheon engagement in an hour. At the Diogenes Club.'

Chapter Eight
The Diogenes Club

A visit to the Diogenes Club could mean only one thing: a meeting with my friend's remarkable brother, Mycroft, to whom I had first been introduced some eleven years earlier during our investigations into the case of *The Greek Interpreter*, an exploit recorded elsewhere.

Mycroft Holmes possessed the same extraordinary mental faculties as my friend, and indeed, Holmes maintained that his brother's powers of observation and deduction were greater than his own. However, he had no interest in detective work. 'He has no ambition in that direction and certainly no energy to follow up clues, to chase around in order to prove what is, for him, obvious in the first place,' Sherlock Holmes had informed me.

On the occasion when he introduced us to the problem about Melas, the little Grecian interpreter, I had been told that Mycroft audited books in some of the government departments, but, over the years, my knowledge of my friend's brother grew and I came to realise that he had a far more important position than I had at first been led to believe. It became apparent that he had great power in government circles. His singularity of brain, the range and intensity of his knowledge, had gained him an influential voice in deciding our nation's policies and international agreements. It was because of this that I assumed our invitation to lunch had more to do with European politics, and those of Ruritania in particular, that just a social tête à tête or a fraternal reunion.

Within an hour of receiving the telegram Holmes and I were strolling down Pall Mall from the St James's end towards the Diogenes Club as casually and nonchalantly as any two city men on their way to a convivial luncheon appointment. None of the people passing by, if given to such speculation, would have guessed the dangerous secrets we held or the onerous task that was set before us. Indeed, as we walked on that mild autumn day with the faint September breeze in our faces, we must have appeared as two carefree gentlemen out for pre-prandial exercise. I must confess that I felt strangely relaxed and at ease as we neared our destination.

Some little distance from the Carlton is the entrance to the Diogenes Club. It was the queerest club in London, run for the convenience of the most unsociable men in the capital. On the occasion of my first visit, at the start of the Melas affair, Holmes had explained it thus: 'There are many men in London, you know, who, some from shyness, some from misanthropy, have no wish for the company of their fellows. Yet they are not averse to comfortable chairs and the latest periodicals. It is for the convenience of these that the Diogenes Club was started. No member is permitted to take the least notice of any other one. Save in the Strangers' Room, no talking is, under any circumstances, permitted and three offences, if brought to the notice of the committee, render the talker liable to expulsion. My brother was one of the founders and I have myself found it a very soothing atmosphere.'

Like the members, the entrance was discreet and inconspicuous. We mounted a few steps before passing through a plain mahogany door bearing a small brass plate with the club's name, and entered a darkened hall, leaving behind the hustle and bustle of Pall Mall. Through glass panelling I caught a glimpse of a large, luxurious room in which a considerable number of men were sitting about and reading papers, each in his own nook. A thin blue veil of smoke hung in the air, further diffusing the daylight, already restricted by closely drawn heavy drapes. It was as though there was a determined effort to keep the outside world at bay.

We were attended by a dark man in a sombre porter's uniform. Without a word he proffered a silver tray for Holmes, who extracted one of his cards from his waistcoat pocket, scribbled a few words on it and placed it on the tray. The porter departed noiselessly, while my companion led me to a side chamber which I knew to be the Strangers' Room: oak panelled and sparsely furnished. In the corner by the window overlooking Pall Mall was a small table, covered in a crisp white cloth and laid with silver service for three. At the side of this table was an ice bucket on a stand, complete with a napkin-wrapped bottle of wine. As we wandered over to the table, the door swung open behind us.

'Ah, Sherlock, punctual as ever. And Doctor Watson. Good to see you again.'

I turned to see the heavily built frame of Mycroft Holmes advancing towards me with an outstretched hand like a seal's flipper. He gave me a hearty handshake, while I returned his greeting.

At first glance one might make the mistaken observation that the man was bloated and very overweight. There was no doubt he was large, almost corpulent, but his height, which was well over six feet, helped him carry it and there was about him, when he moved, a nimbleness and grace denied most fat men. He was seven years Sherlock Holmes's senior and his cheek pouches were drooping now, like those of an eager bloodhound. His hair was already grizzled grey, matching the colour of his watery, deep-set eyes, shining with that keen awareness I recognised in my friend. Altogether there was an aura about the man that made one forget his size and be conscious only of his superior intellect.

He patted Holmes's arm in brotherly affection. 'I see you have tried that new Arabian blend that Bradley's have started stocking,' he said mischievously, brushing a few flakes of ash from his brother's sleeve.

'And you,' returned Holmes, 'have had a very busy morning.' He pointed at Mycroft's chin. 'Time only for a rough shave. The early morning light is most inadequate when one is in a hurry.'

'True, I have had a very busy morning, mainly on your account, Sherlock. My set daily routine has been thrown into disarray.'

Moving around us towards the table, he gestured for us to take our seats.

'The entertaining of visitors, as you know, is not encouraged, so I can only offer you a cold collation, but to compensate I have had an excellent hock brought up from the cellars with which to wash it down.'

Dexterously he took the bottle from the ice bucket and began to open it. As he extracted the cork two of the club's servants, drafted as waiters for this occasion, entered wheeling in trolleys decked with dishes of various cooked meats and salad dressings. Silently they placed the trolleys so that we could serve ourselves and then, without a word, they made a discreet exit.

'Now then, let us not stand on ceremony. Do help yourselves to this simple fare,' invited Mycroft, who was already piling up his plate.

I have to admit I had not realised how hungry I was until I saw the attractive array of food before me. I had, by now, shaken off the fatigue of a missed night's sleep and the brief stroll in the fresh air had stimulated my appetite.

Whatever it was that Mycroft and Sherlock wished to discuss, neither made any reference to it during the meal. They chatted amicably on a wide range of issues, none of immediate import. It was if they were obeying some unwritten law stating that weighty matters were not to be tackled until some refreshment and a period of light-hearted conversation had been enjoyed.

While we ate the brothers touched on many disparate topics, ranging from the Uitlanders of Transvaal, through Kipling's *Jungle Books*, to mediaeval stringed instruments. Mycroft was in a most convivial mood, and often encouraged me to voice my opinions. With the stimulating conversation, the wine and pleasant company, it was easy for me to forget for a while the dangerous case upon which we were engaged.

After our plates had been pushed to one side and coffee had been served by the two silent waiters, who had magically reappeared at the crucial moment, there was a lull. Holmes and I had indulged in a smoke, while Mycroft took snuff from a tortoiseshell box. Brushing away the wandering grains from his coat with a large red silk handkerchief, he left his chair and gazed out of the window at the passing traffic in Pall Mall.

'You've been up to your old tricks again, Sherlock,' he said at length, in a voice still retaining its conviviality. 'Getting yourself involved in precarious political intrigues.'

My friend gave a dry chuckle. 'On this occasion, my dear Mycroft, the political intrigue came knocking on my door.'

'They always do. But, be that as it may, whenever you take on these issues by yourself, the problems land on my desk.' Mycroft returned to his seat and gave an exasperated snort, but there was an indulgent sparkle in his eye, nevertheless. 'Murdered diplomats in railway hotels, foreign revolutionaries shot in east London, and police inspectors who should know better, getting themselves wounded by helping in your researches.'

I was astounded that Mycroft knew so much of what had happened to us while we had followed up the various threads in the Ruritanian affair. If I needed confirmation of his importance and omniscience, here it was. Holmes, however, showed no surprise at his brother's knowledge.

Mycroft gave a bleak smile. 'All right, Sherlock, you had better give me all the facts in full, if I'm going to be of any help to you.'

My friend drew on his pipe and released a cloud of smoke to float to the ceiling. 'That's more like it, Mycroft,' said he with some satisfaction and, settling back in his chair, he proceeded to give a concise, but complete, account of our adventures since the arrival of Colonel Sapt at our Baker Street rooms the previous evening until the departure of Lord Burlesdon and his son an hour or so before.

Throughout Mycroft listened attentively, his expression betraying nothing, and, when Holmes had finished, he remained silent for some time. It was as though his methodical brain was sorting out and docketing all the evidence before assembling the vital elements into a summative conclusion. As he thought his face was immobile, but his deep-set eyes took on that faraway, introspective look which I had seen so often in his brother when he was exerting his full powers.

'I must thank you, Sherlock, for your balanced review. Some aspects of the Ruritanian situation I knew of already, of course. We have been monitoring the volatile situation there for some time. Small country though it is, Ruritania is an old ally of ours and very much a stabilising influence in middle Europe where, in this century, monarchy as a traditional system of government has suffered many keen blows and now is a most vulnerable and beleaguered institution. We know of Count Rupert of Hentzau, his nefarious ambitions and of the infirmity of King Rudolf V. Sir Jasper Meek has briefed us about his "illness".'

He paused to indulge himself with more snuff before returning to his theme.

'However, Rassendyll's substitution at the Coronation and his impersonation of the King is surprising news indeed. This is a secret that must be safely guarded. If the facts become public knowledge, they could rock the very foundations of European politics. That the Elfberg heir to the throne was replaced at his Coronation by an English commoner . . . that Rudolf has never been crowned . . . I tell you, gentlemen, there is more than one country with a regime ruthless enough to take unfair advantage of such information. Invasion, even war, might not be out of the question. It is in Britain's interests that any stories or rumours concerning the insecurity of the Ruritanian monarchy should be quashed immediately.'

'It would seem,' commented Holmes, 'that the major hazard lies not so much in these revelations, but how such knowledge might be used. This focuses on the real threat: Count Rupert. His motivation is fired by the highest ambition – to oust the Elfberg line and establish himself as the first of a new dynasty. I believe he means to bring this about in the most subtle of *coups d'état*.'

Mycroft's eyes shone fiercely with concentration at his brother's words. He leant forward in rapt attention.

'As I read the situation,' Holmes continued, 'Count Rupert means to substitute Rassendyll for the King once more, eliminating Rudolf in the process. Then, after some little time, when the substitution has proved effective, Rassendyll's usefulness as a puppet-king will be over. "King Rudolf" will proclaim his abdication, probably because of his ill-health, and then he will declare his successor – his "close friend and ally" Count Rupert of Hentzau.'

'My God,' I exclaimed. 'How will he get away with it?'

'Who will be there to stop him?'

'When do you think Rupert will make his first move,' asked Mycroft.

'It seems likely that he will attempt to present the impostor king during the State Visit of the King of Bohemia. That is due to start in five days' time.'

'Surely,' I interposed, 'Rassendyll only has to learn of his nephew's safety for him to refuse to act for Rupert?'

Both brothers shook their heads, but it was Mycroft who spoke.

'Now that Rassendyll is in Ruritania it will not be as simple as that. If he tries to go against Rupert's wishes, he could be hauled into the public eye and exposed as the King's impostor and the Queen's lover. This would, of course, place Flavia's life in jeopardy also and plunge the country into turmoil. Just such a situation would ideal for Rupert to sweep to power.'

'You see, Watson,' said Sherlock Holmes, 'how very tangled is the skein fate has elected us to unravel.'

'Just so,' I replied, feeling somewhat despondent after hearing the brothers' words and realising with greater clarity the full ramifications of the problem.

'What is your plan of campaign?' enquired Mycroft.

'I must follow the only lead we have. Watson and I travel to Ruritania tonight. Once there I hope to contact Fritz von Tarlenheim, a confidant of Sapt and Rassendyll.'

Mycroft nodded. 'I know of him. With Sapt gone he is the nearest to the Queen in loyalty. This is a most desperate game you are playing, Sherlock.'

'But one I must play – to the end!'

'On this occasion, I am bound to agree with you. Official forces

cannot be used in this matter. It needs more delicate and surrep-
titious handling.' He gave a brief, mirthless laugh. 'If any man can do
it, I know you can.'

'Thank you,' acknowledged Holmes quietly.

'And the trusty Watson is going too, eh?'

'I am lost without my Boswell.'

'Indeed you are, but this is one exploit that you will not be able to
prepare for publication, Doctor. Not in our lifetime, at least.'

I bowed my head to him. 'There are greater issues of concern here
than author's royalties.'

'You are a good man, Watson. I have heard my brother say there is
no-one he would rather have at his side in a crisis. Our brief meetings
have strengthened my belief in his sentiments.'

I was touched by the great man's sincerity and I thanked him.

Mycroft pulled a long, buff envelope from an inside pocket and
offered it to his brother, saying, 'Here, then, are the documents
you requested in your telegram. Papers of passage for yourself and
Watson under the names of Hawkins and Murray and a letter of
introduction to Sir Roger Johnson, the British Ambassador in Strelsau. Not the brightest of fellows, unfortunately, but it will do him
good to be shaken out of his malaise. He's been vegetating in the
Embassy there for five years or so. It's hardly the most taxing of
appointments. I'll cable him of your arrival and ask him to have one
of his servants meet you from the train. Sir Roger will be able to
arrange direct access for you to Tarlenheim and Queen Flavia.'

'Excellent,' said Holmes, taking the envelope and slipping it into
his coat.

'When do you leave?'

'On the 5.15 from Charing Cross. We should be in Strelsau in
about thirty-six hours, after a brief wait for a connection in Cologne.'

'Is there any further assistance I can give you?'

Holmes patted his pocket. 'You have given me the essentials.'

'Then all I can offer you both are my good wishes,' said Mycroft,
rising from his chair and extending his hand toward us. 'There is
more than the security of the Elfberg monarchy at stake and both
Her Majesty's Government and I await the outcome of your mission
with deep concern.'

We shook hands and made our way to the door, but Mycroft
delayed our exit with one final comment. 'Remember that Rupert
of Hentzau is a wily and determined character. He cannot be over-
estimated. I beg you, be on your guard at all times.'

Some moments later, two gentlemen emerged from the Diogenes Club into the pale autumn sunlight. Mr Hawkins and Mr Murray were taking their first steps on what was to be the most perilous mission of their lives.

Chapter Nine
The journey

By six o'clock that evening Holmes and I were sitting in our own first-class compartment on the South Eastern Continental Express as it steamed through the Kent countryside on its way to Dover – where we were to catch the late-evening ferry to Ostend – the first leg of our journey to Strelsau. The day was fading fast and the setting sun cast streaks of gold across the hop fields.

Since our return to Baker Street Holmes had busied himself in preparation for the trip, consulting maps and gazetteers and perusing his newspaper files and various reference volumes. He had also assembled an odd collection of items from his chemical shelves and his make-up case to take with him. There had been little for me to do save pack my case and prepare myself mentally for the journey. I browsed through the daily papers in a desultory fashion until I came across an item in the Stop Press in the afternoon edition of the *Westminster Gazette*:

RURITANIAN DIPLOMAT DIES OF HEART ATTACK

The body of a Ruritanian diplomat, Colonel Helmut Sapt (58), was discovered this morning in his room at the Charing Cross Hotel by a chambermaid. Medical opinion is that he died of a heart attack.

I pointed this out to my friend.
'Mycroft's work,' said he succinctly.
Now that we had left London behind Holmes appeared relaxed, seated by the carriage window, smoking a cigarette and looking out at the landscape where the trees and hedges were slowly merging with the growing dusk.
I consulted my timetable and my pocket watch. 'Another hour and ten minutes and we'll be in Dover,' I announced.
Holmes nodded and took the cigarette from his mouth. 'Watson,

we have quite a way to go yet. I do hope you will not be issuing regular time checks on our progress.'

'Of course not,' I replied grumpily, snapping down the cover on my hunter.

'Relax, old friend, we are on the easiest part of our mission. There is no point in wearing out our nerves now. They will be sorely tested later, I vouchsafe. For the time being we are in the capable hands of those who run this railway network. Let us leave the worry to them, while we take it easy.'

'Of course,' I replied, still a little hurt by Holmes's barb.

We spent the rest of the journey in silence. Holmes dropped off to sleep after finishing his cigarette and I stared out of the window, watching the inexorable sealing up of the day.

At Dover we transferred to the ferry. It was an uneventful, if uncomfortable, crossing. Because of our relatively late booking we were unable to procure a first-class cabin and we spent the night in cramped quarters. Holmes has a remarkable facility for doing without sleep as long as it is necessary for him so to do and also being able to sleep anywhere or any time he wanted. While I lay, cold and uncomfortable, gazing open-eyed at the gently rolling ceiling, he purred softly in the deepest slumber.

Morning saw us once more travelling by rail. Having left Ostend we were *en route* for Cologne to pick up the Golden Lion Express which would take us, via Dresden, to Strelsau. Shortly after leaving Ostend we repaired to the dining car where we ate a hearty breakfast. As we lazed over our coffee at the end of the meal, I decided to question Holmes about his plans once we reached our final destination.

'Any plans must, at this stage, be tentative. There are so many unknown factors to contend with in this affair, but there are certain objectives which must be achieved as soon as possible. Tarlenheim and Queen Flavia must be informed without delay of the ramifications of Rupert's plot. It is also essential that we discover Rassendyll's whereabouts.'

'Surely the headquarters of the Blues at the castle at Zenda is the most likely location?'

'Possibly,' said Holmes thoughtfully. 'Maybe that would be a trifle obvious and therefore not really Rupert's style at all. Rassendyll is his trump card and the sleeve where he is hidden must be less than obvious. We must also learn from the Queen the planned arrangements for the King of Bohemia's visit. That information will – '

My companion broke off abruptly as the waiter returned to replenish our cups. '*Est-ce que le petit déjeuner vous a plu?*' he enquired.

'*Très bien,*' rejoined Holmes, who said nothing further until the waiter was out of earshot . . . 'I think it would be wise to reserve any further discussion until later in the privacy of our compartment. We do not know how many ears may be straining to catch our words.'

I surveyed the dining-car cautiously. Every occupant was innocently engaged in consuming breakfast or conversing with fellow-travellers. They all appeared respectable and nondescript, but, of course, that is how a clever spy would appear. Indeed, Holmes and I were a case in point: neither of us gave any indication of his true identity or the real purpose behind his journey.

When we returned to our compartment I asked Holmes if he really did believe we were being watched. He looked at me noncommitally. 'I don't really know, Watson, but remember Mycroft's parting words,' he replied, before flopping down in the seat by the window to attend to his first pipe of the day. I settled opposite him, somewhat disheartened at the prospect of a long tedious day of inaction. My mind was too preoccupied to read or discuss any other topic but the Ruritanian question. Holmes himself was disinclined to converse and, having purchased several newspapers at the Ostend terminus, he spent his time perusing them at length.

It was late in the afternoon when we steamed into Cologne, where we were to change to the Golden Lion Express. We had been delayed by line workings in the suburbs and, as a result, there was only a short time at our disposal to cross the station to make our connection.

Cologne station was a high, gloomy, rather neglected building, crammed with hordes of travellers. We left the train clasping our luggage and began making our way through the bustling crowd to Platform 5, where the Golden Lion would be waiting. Conscious of our lack of time, we forged ahead with a will, until, above the echoing noise of chatter, the calls of the porters, the hiss of escaping steam and the screams of train whistles, I heard the sound of a commotion in the crowd behind us. I turned to see what was causing the fuss when a burly young rough, thrusting his way through the mass of people, barged into me, temporarily knocking me off balance. As I staggered sideways, he grabbed the case from my uncertain grasp and made off with it.

'*Haltet den Dieb!*' cried a voice back in the crowd.

Without a word Holmes and I gave chase to the young thief who was already starting to merge into the throng of travellers. With great agility he darted in and out of the crowd, but after a day of rest and inaction, we were fresh and easily able to keep up with him. The majority of the people hardly gave a moment's glance to the three of us as we brushed past them.

This kind of baggage-snatching must, I reflected, be a common occurrence here, as it was in London's great termini. The weary and often slightly bewildered traveller was easy prey for the practised young villain with speed and familiarity of terrain on his side. As we ran, I must admit, my concern was less for my luggage and more for the danger of missing our connection. Later I, and even Holmes, had to admit that we gave chase through an automatic instinct rather than a reasoned decision.

The crowd thinned out as we moved away from the main section of the station and we were able to increase our speed and gain on the young ruffian. As he plunged further into an isolated part of the station, he threw a fleeting glance behind him before leaping over a barrier and sprinting off into the gloom. We followed suit and found ourselves in a dingy area of the station that appeared to be used for unloading goods wagons, which were lined up down several otherwise deserted platforms. The illumination was much dimmer here, but the sound of running feet kept us on the trail of our quarry. As we got within twenty feet of him, he swerved to his left past a silent locomotive down a narrow platform, lit only at intervals by yellow pools spilled by a series of feeble gas lights. To the left were the hulking shadows of a line of goods wagons and to the right a brick wall. He was slowly hemming himself in.

Then suddenly he did something that was totally unexpected. Halfway down the platform he stopped running and swivelled on his heels to face us. As he did so the youth's features were caught in one of the circles of light. He was smiling.

Immediately Holmes grabbed my arm and pulled me up short. 'Quick,' he hissed, dragging me out of the light over to the wall and behind a large packing case abandoned in the shadows. Little rodents scurried away at our approach. Without a word, Holmes drew my attention to the top of the platform where we had just passed. Emerging from the darkness, by the engine, were four vicious-looking louts, each brandishing some kind of cosh or bludgeon. It was a chilling tableau.

'A trap, Watson.'

The shock of realisation came with crystal clarity. The theft of my luggage had been used to decoy us away from the main part of the station to this deserted stretch, so we could be dealt with by this unholy crew.

As the four men advanced with menacing slowness our young thief dropped my case at his feet and pulled a weapon from his belt. I caught the flash of a blade in his hand. In the meantime, Holmes had crouched down and opened his travelling bag from which he extracted a small object.

'Now then, Watson,' he whispered urgently, 'do you think you can tackle the lad and retrieve your case?'

'I'm willing to try,' I replied earnestly.

'Good man!'

'But what about those other blackguards?'

He cast a quick look in the direction of the ugly quartet who were still moving slowly down the platform towards us. 'I think I can handle them with the aid of this little toy.' He held up the familiar grey object. 'Now, when I give the word, you rush the lad, grab your case and slip over the edge of the platform, find your way under the couplings and cross to the adjacent platform.'

'What about you?'

'With luck, I shall not be far behind you. Ready?'

'Yes.'

'Right!'

With an ear-splitting yell Holmes tossed the smoke rocket towards the would-be assassins. It landed and burst about a yard before them. After a spray of sparks, thick clouds of smoke spiralled up before their astonished eyes. I was already darting from the shadows towards the youth with my case when I heard their cries of bewilderment and terror. So disconcerted by the confusion and the advancing grey swirls was my target that he simply dropped his knife and ran.

To the sounds of choking gasps and stumbling feet, I grabbed my case and dived over the edge of the platform. Here the air was untainted by the smoke and I took a gulp of it before feeling my way down the goods wagon until I came to the buffers. By crouching low I was able to slip under the couplings and scramble into the gap between the tracks. Once there, after catching my breath, I had to negotiate the buffers of another goods wagon on the next set of tracks before I reached the far platform.

As I clambered up I was joined by Holmes and, moments later, a little dishevelled by our exertions, but otherwise none the worse for the little *divertissement* specially arranged for us (we had no doubt) by the Blues, we were back in the main body of the station, heading for Platform 5. Holmes was chuckling merrily as we hurried to catch our connection. 'Oh, Watson, we were a little slow to begin with, but they were so very clumsy.'

'Well, it certainly proves that they know of our mission.'

'Yes, and what interests me most of all is how they came by that knowledge. Still, there is one aspect of this incident that is rather satisfying.'

'And what is that?'

'We have them worried. So worried that they feel the need to have us killed.'

I considered this a rather dubious consolation.

We were only just in time for our train. The guard was blowing his whistle for departure when we boarded the Golden Lion and, as we tumbled into a compartment, we were already speeding eastwards over the Rhine on the last stage of our journey.

* * *

With the darkness came the rain. It lashed ferociously against our carriage window as we sped into the night.

'One has never experienced a thunderstorm until caught in one of the continental variety,' remarked my companion, as a flash of lightning lit up the distant hills, followed seconds later by a booming crash of thunder which seemed to shake the carriage. The downpour continued for most of the night. It was only after we had passed through Dresden, where we had an hour's wait, that the rain showed signs of abating.

It was still dark when at last we reached the Ruritanian frontier. Here all passengers had to leave the train and enter the Customs House to have their papers checked and stamped. We were marshalled into the rather rustic-looking building by border guards. The old officer who presided over the Customs House was a slow and meticulous fellow and the delay caused by his assiduity angered some fellow-passengers. However, he, who must have experienced many such shows of impatience, took no notice and continued in his unhurried and methodical fashion.

When it came to our turn he seemed particularly cautious, scrutinising our documents with extreme care. He asked what was the purpose of our visit to his country. 'We are on a walking holiday,' Holmes claimed blandly.

Taking our papers with him he disappeared into an office behind him, much to the dismay of those waiting in the queue. He emerged some minutes later and beckoned us round the corner and into his own office.

Once inside, the door closed behind us and we came face to face with a slim, smooth-faced young man with startling blue eyes. He was dressed in a short double-breasted black coat with an astrakhan collar and he carried a silver-topped cane. He addressed the customs officer, 'Thank you, Stephan, you may leave us.'

The old man bowed and left. At his departure the young man stiffly turned to us with a serous smile and an outstretched hand. 'Mr Hawkins and Mr Murray, I presume. Or would you rather I refer to you as Dr Watson and Mr Holmes?' He gave a curt bow.

I felt a tensing of my nerves at this address and automatically my hand strayed into my pocket for my revolver. Holmes did not reply to the young man's jaunty question, but raised a quizzical eyebrow.

The stranger responded. 'Forgive me. I am Alexander Beauchamp, aide to the British Ambassador in Strelsau. I have been sent by him to waylay you at the frontier. Our intelligences inform us that there is likely to be a welcoming party for you, arranged by Count Rupert of Hentzau, once you step off the train in the capital.'

'We've already had a taste of their hospitality in Cologne,' I said, relieved at his identification, and shook his hand.

Beauchamp's face registered surprise. 'You have been set upon already? Great heavens, I had no idea they would spread their net so wide. Thank goodness you are safe.'

'Thank you for your concern,' said Holmes with a brief smile. 'Now it seems that my friend and I are in your hands. What do you propose?'

'I have a coach waiting outside for us. We will drive to a little inn, the Boar's Head, just five miles this side of Strelsau. I have engaged rooms for you there . . . in your *noms de guerre*, of course.' He allowed himself a little smile before continuing. 'Later this morning Sir Roger will visit you for consultation.'

'It appears as though it has all been most efficiently organised.'

'Very well, gentlemen,' said Beauchamp. 'If you are ready we shall leave at once.'

He led us out through the rear of the Customs House into the cool air of the Ruritanian dawn. It was still too dark to see our surroundings clearly as we boarded a small, nondescript coach for our journey.

While the great express train panted steam impatiently, waiting for the custom check to be completed, the coach struck out at speed for the Boar's Head.

Chapter Ten
The Boar's Head

As we travelled towards the Boar's Head I was unable to be fully at ease. Alexander Beauchamp was a personable and considerate young man, but I felt uncomfortable in his presence. It was not clear to Holmes or myself just how much he was cognisant of the matters in hand. Did he know the purpose of our mission and of Rassendyll's abduction? Did he know of Rupert's plot to usurp the throne? There was no way of knowing and so we were unable to discuss the situation with him or even between ourselves. He, too, seemed reluctant to make references to Count Rupert or to our forthcoming meeting with Sir Roger, the British Ambassador, therefore our conversation was fitful and generalised.

However, Beauchamp did tell us something of his background. He had a Ruritanian mother and a French father, but had been educated in England. Holmes smiled pleasantly at this volunteered information, but I could tell from his expression that, despite this apparent display of interest, his mind was engaged elsewhere.

Apart from these occasional bursts of conversation, most of our two-hour journey was spent in silence, with Holmes lost in thought and Beauchamp sitting back in his seat chain-smoking small black cheroots. He offered them to Holmes and me. I declined, but my companion accepted and soon the coach was filled with pungent odours.

Dawn gradually broke, giving me a first glimpse of the Ruritanian countryside. Autumn was more advanced here than in England and the trees were ablaze with vibrant colours highlighted by the rays of the rising sun. Our route was by a series of rough country roads, some of which were little more than cart tracks, winding their way mainly through woodland. At one point we skirted a large area of water.

'That is Lake Teufel,' Beauchamp told us. 'The legend is that the Devil's brother lives at the bottom of the lake and one day he will rise up and flood the whole of our country.' He chuckled gently.

'There are some woodland peasants who really believe this story and, although it is rich in fish – the largest carp you have ever seen – the lake is avoided by the natives. The old King had a fishing-lodge there, but since his death it has fallen into disuse.'

Holmes stirred himself from his reverie to peer down at the grey stretch of water edged by the thick forest, only interrupted at the far side of the lake by the dark outline of the lodge which Beauchamp had mentioned.

'That, I take it, is the Forest of Zenda?'

'Yes,' replied our companion. 'Beyond that rise is the castle.'

Holmes continued to gaze out and observe the scene until the lake was screened from our sight by the sweep of yet more trees.

Towards seven o'clock we approached the brow of a hill. Perched at the top was was a large white-washed building, stained at intervals by the spread of ivy clinging to its walls. A sign proclaimed this to be our destination: the Boar's Head. As we drew closer it was easy to appreciate why this place had been chosen as our rendezvous, for there were no other buildings nearby. On reaching the crest of the hill we saw, spread out below, peeping through the matitutinal mist, the great city of Strelsau, capital of Ruritania. The dome and spires of its cathedral, the highest points in the city, glowed red as they pierced the grey vapours.

When we alighted from the coach, the rough wooden door of the inn swung open and a florid-faced fellow in a white apron greeted us with a wave.

'That is Gustav, the landlord,' murmured Beauchamp. 'He knows you only as important guests.'

We were given an effusive welcome by our host and shown into the inn, where the air was stale and chill. The driver brought our luggage, supervised by Beauchamp, who then instructed Gustav to show us our rooms. With smiles and gestures he led us up a wide staircase running up from the centre of the inn on to a kind of minstrels' gallery and from there into a simple but spacious suite. Here a table was laid for breakfast, with cold meats and cheeses. In the grate a log fire, recently lit, was struggling into a blaze.

While Gustav hurried away for coffee, we flung our coats off and settled down at the table for our meal. Beauchamp examined his watch. 'It is seven fifteen now. The Ambassador should be here in another hour.'

Breakfast was pleasant enough, but cold fare at that time of day is not really to my liking. However, the coffee was scalding hot and reviving. Afterwards we smoked, Holmes and I our pipes and Beau-champ his cheroots. At his request I regaled him with a full account of our Cologne station adventure, while Holmes sat back, eyes closed, in a meditative posture. Beauchamp listened with attention, his blue eyes fixed in concentration and, at the end of my account, he app-eared both fascinated and full of admiration for Holmes's presence of mind.

'That is an amazing story, Dr Watson. Of course, I realise that it would not be diplomatic for me to enquire as to why Count Rupert is so keen to eliminate you. I do know that he has created many enemies since his return to the country, especially at the Court, and there are many rumours concerning his ruthless behaviour and craving for power, but I never realised until now that his influence had spread beyond the borders of Ruritania. As your story confirms that this is the case, it would seem not unrealistic to suppose that Rupert was in some way responsible for the murder of Colonel Sapt in London.'

Before I was able to comment, Holmes leant forward and addressed Beauchamp. 'It is not beyond the bounds of possibility, certainly. But tell me, Beauchamp, to come to more pressing matters, where else, apart from the castle at Zenda, does Count Rupert have private quarters?'

'Oh, that I do not know.'

'Are there no rumours which suggest some location?'

Beauchamp shook his head. 'None that I have heard.'

Holmes stood up and wandered over to the window, flung it open and took a breath of the morning air before returning to where Beauchamp was sitting. 'That is a pity,' he said sadly. 'I really did think that one of Rupert's right-hand men would have been en-trusted with such information by his master. Especially someone as close to the Count as you, Baron Holstein.'

Beauchamp leapt to his feet, his hand darting towards the inside pocket of his jacket, but Holmes was too quick for him and delivered a quick, fierce uppercut to his jaw. He fell back in his seat, out cold.

'What on earth is going on?' I asked in bewilderment.

'Just preventing the Baron from using his little weapon,' replied Holmes, pulling from the inside of Beauchamp's jacket a small Derringer pistol. 'An unreliable weapon with a penchant for jam-ming at the vital moment, as well as having a holster that produces a most telling bulge to the jacket.'

'Then Beauchamp is our enemy?'

'This man,' said Holmes, indicating the inert figure before us, 'is Baron Heinrich Holstein, late of the Ruritanian cavalry and one of the Count of Hentzau's closest confidants. He is also the assassin of Colonel Sapt.'

'What!' I gasped. 'How can you be certain of this?'

'You remember the name Holstein?'

'Of course. You heard it mentioned by "Checked Cap" at the house in Burdett Road.'

'Exactly. And the kidnapper who visited Lord Burlesdon had a cigar case inscribed with the initials "H. H". He also smoked black cheroots, as does our acquaintance here, and so did the murderer of Colonel Sapt. If you recall, I remarked that the killer had enjoyed a smoke after the cruel deed. The ash he left behind was an unmistaable type and easily identifiable to my trained eye. Also in the ashtray in Sapt's room I found a spent match that he had used to light his cheroot. It was snapped in two. Beauchamp exhibited the same idiosyncratic habit of breaking the matchstick after use. Even when I accepted a light from him in the coach he snapped the match before throwing it from the window. The cigar case which he proferred me has a strip of black tape along the corner: this was obviously to block out his carved initials. It was these that led me in my research back in Baker Street to the name of Heinrich Holstein, a scion of the Ruritanian house of Holstein, one of the lesser noble dynasties of this country. Holstein served in the royal cavalry until three years ago, when he left suddenly, under rather a cloud.'

Holmes reached into Holstein's pocket and retrieved the cigar case. Pulling back the strip of tape he revealed the initials 'H. H', as he had surmised.

'Although the tape covered the initials, it did not mask the insignia here.' Holmes pointed to the opposite corner of the case where there was a motif of an eagle perched on a sceptre. 'The family arms of the Holsteins.'

'All this information you gleaned before we left England?' I asked with some astonishment.

'Yes. But there were two further indiscretions giving further proof that we were dealing with an enemy agent. He referred to Sapt's murder. Only those directly concerned with the Colonel's death could know it was not natural: the official story that was given out, you will recall, was that he died of heart failure.'

'What was Holstein's other slip?'

'Examine the stick Holstein carried,' said Holmes, handing me the silver-topped cane. I scrutinised it carefully, but could see nothing incriminating about and said so.

'Look closely at the silver top, Watson – the filigree decoration.'

'Finely worked. An inscribed flower design.'

'What flower?'

'Ah,' I exclaimed, realisation dawning upon me. 'The blue bugle!'

'Precisely.'

'The nerve of the man!'

'Indeed. His arrogance never allowed him to suspect that such minutiae would be observed by someone who, by means of deductive reasoning, could interpret those details and reach the truth.'

Before my friend was able to continue, there came a sudden heavy knock at the door. We exchanged concerned glances.

'Quick,' said Holmes softly, 'stand in front of Holstein so that he cannot be seen from the door and appear to be talking to him.'

I did as Holmes asked while he went to answer the door. On opening it he discovered Gustav on the threshold.

'We are rather involved in important private discussions at the moment. Please come back later,' ordered Holmes.

Gustav's florid face, which seemed to have lost some of its joviality, peered into the room over Holmes's shoulder to where I was apparently in animated conversation with Holstein. The landlord looked reluctant to leave and hesitated in the doorway. As he did so Holstein stirred, his eyelids fluttering, and he uttered a muffled moan. Gustav stiffened at this, almost pressing against Holmes to gain a better view into the apartment.

Holstein groaned again. 'I quite agree,' I said quickly, apparently replying to a mumbled comment and I clapped him on the shoulder in friendly agreement. I then turned to face Gustav, still ensuring that I masked his sight from the unconscious Holstein. 'Do leave us, landlord. We have pressing matters to discuss.'

With reluctance Gustav left us.

Just as the door closed, Holstein's eyes blinked open as full consciousness flooded back to him. He gripped the arms of the chair to pull himself to his feet as his mouth opened to cry for assistance. Before he could utter a sound I hit him a fierce blow to the chin and he slumped back into the chair, knocked senseless once more.

'Good man, Watson,' said Holmes. 'At least his attempt to call for help confirms that he has friends here and his friends are our enemies. Therefore we have but little time before they act against us. Help me tie him up and gag him.'

Using a napkin as a gag and some ripped sheets as a rope, we bound Holstein securely to the chair.

'What now?' I asked.

'We must make our escape. As we cannot depart with dignity by the way we came in,' he paused and moved over to the window, 'this must be our exit.'

I joined him at the window. There was a drop of some twenty-five feet to the stable yard below. Holmes indicated a growth of creeper clinging to the wall a few feet to the left of the window.

'We will use that as our ladder. I'm afraid it will mean leaving our cases as they will hamper our progress. However, I must retain my travelling bag as it contains too many items which may prove invaluable before our sojourn in Ruritania is over.'

'Not more smoke rockets?' I grinned.

'A touch – a distinct touch, Watson.'

Swiftly and silently we set about our escape. Holmes went first. With great agility he swung out of the window on to the ivy and slipped to the ground effortlessly. He beckoned me to follow, but before I did so, I dropped his bag down to him. He caught it nimbly.

As I was heavier than my friend, the ivy was less tolerant of my weight and, before reaching the ground, I had to jump as the foliage tore away from the wall.

We hurried into the ramshackle stable at the far side of the yard. Luck was on our side, for inside we found two horses idly munching hay. Although they looked unkempt and rather decrepit, they were a means of escape. After a brief survey of the stable we found some passable harnesses and a couple of ancient saddles and prepared the horses for riding. We then led them round the side of the inn, only yards from the road, before mounting.

'Now, Watson, are you ready for a swift gallop?' enquired Holmes with a twinkle in his eye.

'As swift as these old nags can give us,' I replied, for certainly our mounts appeared to be far from fleet-of foot.

Holmes pointed down the hill. 'To Strelsau – there to seek the residence of the British Ambassador.'

We galloped off together and I soon discovered that the horses' appearance was deceptive. Whether it was that they were grateful for the exercise or that my knowledge of horseflesh was more limited than I believed, I know not, but they surged down the track at great speed.

As we reached the bottom where the landscape levelled out, Holmes raised his hand and brought me to an untidy halt.

'What is it?'

His long arm stretched out and pointed down the road ahead of us. 'Do you see that small cloud of dust in the distance?'

'Yes.'

'Riders heading this way at speed. It would be rather ironic, would it not, if, after all our efforts, we rode straight into a pack of the Blues.'

'You think it is the Blues?'

'Most likely. On their way to pick up two captives at the Boar's Head, I'd say. It would be politic for our safety for us to dismount and secrete ourselves behind that clump of bushes over there until the riders have passed – whoever they may be.'

We did as Holmes suggested and, moments later, we could actually hear the pounding of hooves. As they approached we crept forward on our stomachs to gain a view of the horsemen as they rode by.

There were eight of them and I felt a chill of excitement as they came into view, dressed in their light blue uniforms. But it was their leader, cantering some distance ahead of the rest, who arrested my attention. He was erect in the saddle, his military hat raked at a jaunty angle. Beneath it was a cruel face: despite a thin mouth, which seemed fixed in a cold, mocking smile, the eyes were ruthless and hard.

'That,' whispered Holmes, 'is Rupert of Hentzau.'

Chapter Eleven
Rupert of Hentzau

The city of Strelsau betrayed its mediaeval origins in its ancient architecture and narrow cobbled streets. Although late in the nineteenth century, the stamp of our modern age seemed to have made little impression here. As Sherlock Holmes and I rode through the arched gateway of the capital shortly after eight o'clock that morning we were struck by the quaintness of our surroundings: the part-timbered dwelling houses all crowded together, apparently leaning over the street to greet one another, and the mellow stone buildings adorned with ornate carvings, all untouched by the grime of smoke and fog that besmirches so many of London's edifices.

Despite the early hour there was a sense of bustle and activity. The city was awake and fully engaged in the new day. We were able to merge easily with the growing streams of city folk as they went about their business. We left our horses for a well-earned rest and a bag of hay at a livery stable by the gate. It was here that we enquired of the groom directions to Friedrichstrasse, the location of the British Embassy. Duly directed, we found ourselves on the doorsteps of the smart little building some fifteen minutes later.

Holmes gave his card to the lackey who answered our ring. We were asked to wait in the hall while the servant hurried away to inform his master of our presence. He was gone some minutes before returning to usher us into the Ambassador's office. It was an elegantly appointed room: red velvet drapes hung at the windows, Chinese rugs littered the floor, and there were gilt chairs and a large crystal chandelier, sparkling in the morning light.

By the window, standing behind a highly polished desk, was a short, balding man with grey muttonchop whiskers.

'Gentlemen, gentlemen!' he exclaimed at our entrance and hurried to greet us with hearty handshakes. 'Do take a seat.' He indicated chairs by the fire. Holmes took Mycroft's letter from his coat and handed it to Sir Roger, who sat opposite us with his short legs stretched out in front of him as he perused the document in a perfunctory manner.

'I must confess I am all confusion, gentlemen.' He gave a fussy cough. 'You must realise that usually my duties here in Strelsau are purely of a diplomatic nature and, as such, they are quite routine. Plots, spies, and missing agents are quite out of my realm of experience.'

Holmes smiled sympathetically, but his eyes exhibited no warmth.

'Well, well,' continued our host, 'you both seem none the worse for your late arrival. Perhaps you would care to relate what caused your delay.'

'Watson is the storyteller,' returned my friend, rather brusquely.

'Ah, quite,' said Sir Roger and turned his attention to me with an expectant raise of the eyebrow. Briefly I recounted the details of our journey from our exploit at Cologne station to our undignified departure from the Blue Boar. While I did so, Holmes impatiently paced the room, his brows knotted in frustration.

'My word,' said the Ambassador when I had concluded, 'what an extraordinary tale. And you feel sure that Count Rupert of Hentzau is behind this villainy?'

'Absolutely certain,' snapped Holmes coldly.

'Really! I knew, of course, he was causing the King some problems, but I never realised it was quite this serious. However, after receiving the somewhat cryptic wire from Mr Mycroft Holmes, I went myself to the station this morning to meet the Golden Lion and, when you were not on it, I feared the worst.' He ran his hand across his brow. 'I know it is rather early in the day, but with all this upset, I feel I could do with a spot of brandy. I hope you will join me and then perhaps we can discuss what help I can give you. Now if you'll just excuse me?' With that he rose and hurried from the room.

Holmes's face was icy and immobile.

'What is it, Holmes? You've been acting oddly since we arrived. You were quite rude to Sir Roger.'

'Something is wrong here, Watson. I cannot put my finger on it at the moment, but something is wrong.'

'Don't tell me you have started relying on intuition as a basis for judgement?'

'Certainly not! It is my mind and not my feelings that tell me, but thought processes are sluggish. I cannot extract the reason.' He screwed up his eyes and tapped his brow.

The door opened and Sir Roger Johnson entered, carrying a silver tray on which were three brandy glasses and a bottle. He set it down on his desk.

'This is Ruritanian brandy, blended in the vineyards of Zenda. It has a distinctive taste and is a great reviver.'

Sir Roger poured generous measures for us. 'Let us hope, gentlemen, that there will be no further difficulties to hinder your mission.'

I took a long gulp of the warming liquid and felt the fiery liqueur slip down my throat. Holmes, who had done the same, suddenly gave a sharp cry and threw his glass to the floor.

'Stop, Watson,' he exclaimed, knocking my glass from my hand.

'What is it?'

'I knew there was something,' he said. 'It was the new boots.'

But already his words were fading from my ears and the vibrant colours in the room began to merge before my eyes. The red of the drapes bled into the cream walls and, as I shambled forward, I saw the floor beneath my feet coming towards me. I realised, as a final darkness swept over me, that I had been drugged.

*   *   *

I woke with a start. The sudden shock of icy water on my face left me gasping for air. With great speed I was propelled down a dark tunnel into consciousness. As my vision cleared and my eyes began to focus, I was able to register my surroundings. No longer was I in the opulent chamber at the British Embassy: this new setting was darker and more spartan. The walls, timbered in dark oak, were hung with various animal heads and antique weapons. The pinkish light of evening filtered through the two small windows to my left. Several oil lamps and a blazing log fire set back in a rough stone hearth were the only forms of illumination.

I shook my head in an attempt to clear it of the drug I had taken and to shed the droplets of water still clinging to my face. I saw that I was bound to a wooden carver, as was my friend Sherlock Holmes, who had also been subjected to the cold water treatment. The perpetrator of this, still clutching a dripping pail, was Sir Roger Johnson, whose furtive features were highlighted by the flickering flames.

However, it was the other two occupants of the room who arrested my attention. They stood side by side watching my friend and me with sardonic amusement. I recognised the tall figure and stiff bearing of Baron Holstein, the glow from his cheroot softly lighting his features. The third figure advanced slightly out of the shadows and, although I had only the once glimpsed that cold and cruel visage, I knew it to belong to Count Rupert of Hentzau.

'I am so glad you are awake, gentlemen,' he purred softly. 'Welcome to the King's hunting lodge. I am sorry that His Royal Majesty, King Rudolf, cannot be here in person to greet you, but I'm afraid he has not been in the best of health.' He uttered a brief mirthless chuckle. 'However, his absence is of little consequence, for quite soon I intend to assume ownership, not just of this lodge, you understand, but of all the properties, estates, titles and accoutrements attendant on the King – including the throne of Ruritania.' He beamed in malevolent arrogance, his face alight with that spark of fanaticism I had observed previously in some of our earlier adversaries who had been nourished by some wicked dream. 'I feel sure you will be gratified to know that assisting me in my ascendancy is a fellow countryman of yours: a Mr Rassendyll.'

Holmes continued to remain silent, his mask-like features betraying none of his thoughts or emotions. This lack of reaction annoyed Hentzau, and the smile faded from his lips.

'You have caused me a certain amount of inconvenience, Mr Holmes,' the Count went on, pointing his gloved finger at my friend. 'You interfered badly with my London operation, causing the death of three loyal agents. You slipped my net in Cologne and even managed to evade the clutches of the Baron here.'

Holstein looked coldly at Holmes, but there was anger in the tenseness of his stance.

Rupert of Hentzau resumed. 'However, there is a certain satisfying irony that you were finally brought down in your own Embassy.'

I could no longer remain mute while this blackguard assailed us in this arrogant fashion. I pulled desperately at my bonds without success. 'Another of your impostors and a traitor,' I accused.

'On the contrary, Dr Watson,' replied Rupert silkily, 'Sir Roger is a wise man who knows where his best interests lie.'

I glared with disgust at the turncoat, but he avoided my gaze.

'Don't be too harsh on Sir Roger,' intoned Rupert, 'A bored and lonely man, stuck in a foreign country for many years with little to do . . . he needs a little diversion, a little comfort. And power and money are great persuaders.'

'They are also great corrupters and are especially effective when used by and for those without principle,' remarked Holmes casually.

'Ah, Mr Holmes, I am so glad you have joined us in our little tête à tête. I have, of course, read of your abilities and feel proud that you feel it necessary to journey all the way from London in order for me to wish you goodbye.'

Holmes permitted himself a thin smile. 'I should be a poor specimen indeed were I to allow such an inferior fellow as yourself to bring about the end of my career. Better men than you have tried and failed.'

Hentzau laughed. 'What bravado! Trussed up like a chicken and still believing he has the upper hand. A classic triumph of optimism over reality. The English disease, learned, no doubt, on the playing fields of Eton, Sir Roger?'

The little traitor looked uneasy. 'Let's get on with it. Let's kill them and be done,' he bleated impatiently.

'See how eager he is for your demise, gentlemen. He can hardly wait for your blood to be spilled,' beamed the Count.

'He wants to be rid of us because we are symbols of his own treachery. It is his own cowardly nature that is driving him,' I sneered contemptuously.

My remark ingnited a spark of animal fury in Sir Roger and, with a grunt, the small man stepped forward as if to strike me, but the Count restrained him.

'All in good time. You are not alone in wishing the elimination of our enemies. The Baron here is also keen to see they suffer for their interference.'

Holstein was looking at us through narrowed eyes as he blew a cloud of smoke in our direction. 'My jaw is a little tender,' said he, 'but I do not hold grudges. Death will be a sufficient penalty.'

Rupert of Hentzau grinned at his confederate before turning his mocking gaze on Holmes and me. 'Well, Mr Holmes and Dr Watson, I am afraid it is time for me to depart, but, as you can see, I leave you in good hands. Sadly, I have so many pressing matters to attend to in connection with the arrival of the King of Bohemia in two days' time that I cannot stay to . . . be in at the kill, as it were.'

'Count Rupert,' said Holmes forcefully, 'before you go, I would like to say one thing.'

Our adversary looked puzzled and then flashed his teeth. 'Not your last words?' He threw back his head in a full-throated roar of laughter. 'Take note of these, Baron, we can have them inscribed on his headstone.'

Holmes appeared neither angry nor dismayed by Rupert's response.

'Well, detective, what have you to say?' Hentzau said at length, after his amusement had subsided.

'It is this for you to ponder upon. If you take the Crown, how secure will it be? Your own actions have shown the way to usurp the Crown and others can learn and follow by example. Take Holstein here. How long will he be content to remain your minion? "The love of wicked friends converts to fear" in such arrangements. You will have to be alert at all times, trusting no-one. And there will always be those supporters of the Elfberg dynasty waiting . . . waiting to snatch back what is rightfully theirs. Stop this mad game now while you have the opportunity. There will be no chance later.'

'A very pretty speech, Mr Holmes. What you don't seem to realise is that I cannot deny my destiny. I was born to rule, to wear the crown of my country. Rudolf is a weak and ineffectual king. Ruritania cries out to me. I cannot ignore that call.'

With these words Rupert of Hentzau swept from the room, and moments later we heard his horse galloping away. For some time all remained still in the room, the crackling and spitting of the logs being the only sounds to break the silence.

Baron Holstein was the first to stir. He threw his cheroot into the flames and turned to face Holmes and me. 'Now it's time for a little entertainment,' he announced. His face had lost that youthful earnestness it had exhibited in the coach on the journey to the Blue Boar. It had become a hard and sinister mask.

Sir Roger Johnson still appeared nervous and ill at ease. I felt sure that it was as the full implications of his traitorous act had dawned on him. The promise of money and power had hidden from his greedy eyes the reality of the situation. It was as though he never realised there would be this kind of bloodshed.

'What are you really getting out of this?' I challenged. 'Thirty pieces of silver? Do you think our deaths will be accepted without question in England? There will come others to investigate. Will you kill them also?'

Johnson's face twitched with anxiety in the firelight. 'Let's get this over,' he hissed at Holstein.

'Don't be too impatient, my friend. Those were only the desperate words of a man without hope.' So saying Holstein plunged the poker into the heart of the fire. 'We'll see if these two Englishmen will be as courageous when I've finished with them.'

Sir Roger gave a sharp intake of breath. 'What are you going to do?' he asked tremulously.

Holstein touched his chin. 'They left their mark on me, so I'm only going to return the compliment.'

'You see, Watson,' said Holmes urbanely, 'despite rumours to the contrary, some of the natives here are still barbaric, possessing the mentality of Neanderthal man.'

I could see that he was making these provocative jibes in order to gain time, for, as he spoke, I could see that he was moving his fingers in an attempt to loosen his bonds. However, his efforts were fruitless, his bindings did not budge.

Holstein only chuckled at Holmes's outburst. Pulling the poker from the flames, he held its throbbing tip up before his face, bathing his features in a dull amber glow.

'Now, Mr Holmes, where shall I make my mark?' he said, slowly advancing on my friend.

Chapter Twelve
Queen Flavia

The events that immediately followed Holstein's threatening approach on Sherlock Holmes occurred with such rapidity that, as I
recall them now in my mind, they flicker as images from some kind
of macabre pantomime. It seemed that the Baron was about to brand
the face of my friend with the red-hot poker when, with a suddenness
that made me catch my already bated breath, the door burst open at
the far end of the room. The Baron and Sir Roger both whirled
around at the noise and saw, framed in the doorway, a well-built man
in a military uniform, brandishing a sword.

Without a word he charged into the room towards Holstein who,
in reaction to this imminent danger, hurled the glowing poker at the
stranger. It hit the man's arm and, for an instant, there was the
pungent smell of scorching material before the poker fell to the
floor, there to scar the boards. The stranger was unharmed by the
missile, but the brief hesitation had given Holstein sufficient time to
pull down one of the foils adorning the walls.

Sir Roger cowered in the corner by the fireplace as the men
confronted each other and commenced to lunge and parry with their
swords.

While we watched helplessly as the men, both adept handlers of
the foil, fought, Holmes and I struggled furiously with our bonds.
Tugging strenuously I began to gain more freedom of movement as
the ropes gradually slackened. In my vigorous efforts to pull free,
I almost tipped my chair over: when the little Englishman saw
this, either his fear or his feeble courage, was stimulated enough for
him to grab a short log of firewood from a stack by the grate and
move forward to strike me with it. As he approached Holmes
reacted speedily, thrusting his legs out with great force, causing the
scoundrel to sprawl full length on the floor. Then Holmes, still tied
to the chair, stood up and, with great effort, dragged himself over to
the fireplace. Here he turned around and rammed the back of

the chair against the stonework. He did this twice more in quick succession and, with a groaning, splintering and snapping of wood, the chair began to fall apart.

After one further heave, the arms came adrift from the main body of the chair. By now Sir Roger had clambered unsteadily to his feet, but, with Holmes finally free of constraint, he was able to deliver a well-aimed blow to the treacherous envoy. With a cry he staggered backwards, stumbling into the path of the duellists, just as Holstein was thrusting forward with his rapier. It caught the startled and bewildered traitor just under the heart and, giving a whimper of pain, he crumpled to the floor, clutching his chest.

Holstein was momentarily distracted by this strange turn of events and his opponent was able to lunge at him and pierce him in the arm. He reeled back with a gasp and then, as blood began to seep through the sleeve of his coat, he uttered a frenzied yell of anger and leapt forward to the stranger. It was a gesture guided by fury, rather than skill, and this mistimed action allowed the stranger's foil to find another easy target. Holstein cried out at the hurt of this wound and drew back, crashing into a chair. His opponent advanced with flashing foil.

Now pain and anger controlled Holstein's actions and he slashed wildly, the stranger parrying the attacks with ease, moving relentlessly forward. With a shout of rage, Holstein lunged violently, his foil slicing the air. The stranger nimbly stepped to the side, avoiding the thrust and slipped his sword into the Baron's unprotected midriff.

Holstein's eyes rolled madly in pain and his mouth, moving rapidly, emitted only guttural, choking sounds, as he crashed against the wall. His adversary quickly stepped forward and, with a bitter cry, plunged his weapon into Holstein's breast. With a final rasp of agony the Baron jerked his head back, staring at us with a face creased in pain, but having a twisted, malevolent grin on his lips.

'Farewell,' he croaked, 'a long farewell to all my greatness.' He stumbled a few steps, still brandishing his sword, before sinking to his knees. He gave a bitter, gagging laugh, with blood now trickling from his mouth. Finally he fell face downwards, only feet away from his confederate in treachery.

For some moments there was a silence with no-one moving. It was as though the three of us, Holmes, myself and the stranger, were posing in some bloody tableau. It was the swordsman who eventually broke the silence.

'I am Fritz von Tarlenheim, officer in the service of His Gracious Majesty King Rudolf the Fifth.' He clicked his heels, giving a curt bow.

'We are friends to your cause,' replied Holmes, offering his hand to our champion.

'That I know, sir, or else you would not have been prisoners of Count Rupert.'

'I am Sherlock Holmes.'

'The English detective?'

Holmes gave a nod of acknowledgement.

Tarlenheim grasped Holmes's hand once more and shook it enthusiastically. 'I am most pleased to meet you, sir. I have, of course, read of your genius.'

'And I,' I interposed somewhat brusquely, 'am still tied up, gentlemen.'

Both grinned and Holmes quickly released me.

'This is my friend and biographer, Doctor John Watson,' he introduced, as I found myself free at last and shaking Tarlenheim's hand. 'We are here in Ruritania,' continued Holmes, 'on a mission given to us by your Colonel Sapt. He engaged us in London to discover the whereabouts of Rudolf Rassendyll. Our trail eventually led us to Strelsau.'

'Rassendyll is there in Strelsau?'

'I cannot be sure that he is held in the capital, but he is most certainly in your country.'

Tarlenheim looked both puzzled and alarmed. 'Perhaps, Mr Holmes, you had better tell me your story in full.'

As the flames in the grate dwindled, Sherlock Holmes, with the economy of words and the preciseness of detail that were second nature to him, recounted the essential particulars from Sapt's visit to our rooms up to the moment we were drugged in the Ambassador's residence. When Holmes reached the part in his narrative which dealt with Sapt's murder, Tarlenheim gave an anguished groan and struck the mantelpiece with his fist.

'Rupert will pay for that with his own blood,' he vowed. 'By heavens, even if I have to sacrifice my own life in the process, he'll pay for it!'

For some moments our liberator fought with his mixed emotions of sorrow and anger until he regained his composure and urged Holmes to continue. When Holmes had concluded, Tarlenheim leant against the mantelpiece, staring thoughtfully into the glowing embers.

'The situation is far worse than I imagined,' he said at length. 'I thought we had the covert movements and operations of Rupert and the Blues under strict surveillance. Obviously, I was wrong. However, I am convinced that Rassendyll is not being held in the Castle of Zenda or the Blue Boar Inn or at the Blues' main garrison, the schloss at Berenstein. We have all those places watched around the clock by our agents. As well as this hunting-lodge.'

He turned from the fire to face us. He was a well-built, stocky individual, with a handsome face with broad features adorned by a luxuriant moustache and brown, sensitive eyes.

'Rupert, of late, has taken to holding conferences here at night, since it is not used by the King any more. Of course, it is the scene of his previous triumph. This was the lodge where the King was drugged and eventually kidnapped on his coronation day. It was only last week that I set my men to watch this place from a hide in the woods.' He relaxed his stern features slightly. 'It is the officer on duty to whom you owe your lives, for when he saw Rupert arrive with Holstein, another man and two drugged prisoners, he reported to me at once and I thought it appropriate to investigate.'

'We are extremely grateful that you did,' I assured him.

'Tell me,' interposed Holmes, 'were you already aware of the complicity of Sir Roger Johnson?'

'We suspected as much, but there was no definite proof – or else we would have reported the matter to the British Government and taken action ourselves.'

Instinctively we all looked at the crumpled form of the British Ambassador. There is something inherently sad about a fellow-countryman who has turned his coat and yet I could find no pity in my heart for that unscrupulous little man.

'The fact that Rassendyll is here in Ruritania,' continued Tarlenheim, 'and under constraint to play the King, creates a crisis for us. We have so little time to act. The King of Bohemia arrives in two days' time. What on earth can we do?'

'To begin with, it is imperative that we do not lose heart,' counselled Holmes. 'Our most pressing task is to find where Rassendyll is being guarded by the Blues.'

'Even were we able to do so, how can he help us? If Rassendyll takes any action against Rupert he will be exposed by the Count and the full details of the Coronation scandal will be revealed, destroying all credibility for him and the royal line.'

'Hentzau seems to have us over a barrel,' I remarked gloomily.

Holmes placed his hand reassuringly on Tarlenheim's shoulder. 'Although this is a hazardous and precarious game with, as it would seem, Rupert holding all the aces, Sherlock Holmes still has some trumps to play.'

Holmes's statement eased Tarlenheim's worried features a little. 'Gentlemen,' said he, reaching a decision, 'I suggest we return to the Royal Palace in Strelsau and inform the Queen of the situation.'

*   *   *

I have had an experience of women which extends over many nations and three separate continents, but I can say that I have never seen a woman whose face combined such radiant beauty and graceful serenity as that of Flavia, Queen Consort of Ruritania. Her features were delicate and her skin, which I suspected was naturally pale, had a translucency which radiated loveliness. The albescence of her complexion was further enhanced by the contrasting raven black hair which framed her beautiful face. Her manner was gentle and demure rather than regal, but this added to her attraction. Sherlock Holmes, who seldom takes note of a woman's features other than as a source for deduction, was visibly taken by her appearance.

We met the Queen in her private rooms at the Palace later that same night. Tarlenheim had been engaged with Her Majesty in a private interview for some time before Holmes and I were ushered into her presence. In the meantime Holmes and I had been given quarters of our own and had been able to wash and spruce ourselves up in readiness for our audience with the Queen.

After Tarlenheim had presented us, she took our hands and greeted us warmly. Then, without warning, her mask of friendliness slipped and her features clouded with grief, her eyes growing moist, as she turned away from us to hide her tears.

Tarlenheim looked grimly at us. 'It seems that all good fortune is turning against us, gentlemen. We have this evening received the greatest possible blow. The King is dead.'

'Dead?' I gasped.

'His weakened body finally gave up the fight against his brain fever.'

I groaned involuntarily. Sherlock Holmes said nothing, but I saw that he was as shocked as I was at this tragic turn of events. It was crushing news and seemed to eradicate all hope of successfully defeating Rupert's schemes. Now there was no king and no heir to the throne and there was no obstacle to prevent the Count of

Hentzau, with the power of the Blues behind him, from seizing the kingdom.

Controlling her sobs, the Queen turned back to face us, dabbing her eyes with a lawn handkerchief. 'He was not the man I loved,' she said quietly, almost to herself rather than to us, 'and in recent times he was not even the man I had married, but . . . he was my King.' She closed her eyes for a moment before continuing. 'With Rudolf gone there is no way in which Count Rupert can be prevented –'

Holmes stepped forward. 'Forgive me, Your Majesty, but I believe there is. The death of the King is a considerable setback, I do not deny it, both personally for you and for the Elfberg cause, but it must not deter us in our mission to stop Rupert of Hentzau snatching the Crown and establishing a new dynasty.' His words were spoken softly, but with a firm, persuasive resolution that had almost magical potency. 'We must, at all costs, keep the King's death a secret, for not only will that give us more time to develop our plans and take action against our foes, but also, if the news reached the Blues' camp, it would remove all need to keep Rassendyll alive.'

The Queen's eyes widened in dismay and she put her hand to her mouth to stifle a cry.

'It is true, Your Majesty,' I agreed. 'What need has Rupert of an impostor king when the real king is dead?'

Flavia shook her head sadly. 'What are we to do?' she asked, but, before anyone could reply, she turned suddenly, grasping my friend's arm. 'Fritz tells me you are a very clever and resourceful man, Mr Holmes. Can you aid us?'

'I believe I can,' answered the detective gently. 'If you will allow me to take charge of operations, I have a plan which I am confident can succeed.'

The Queen studied Holmes for a moment and then cast a questioning glance at Tarlenheim who responded quickly, 'I think our only hope is to do as Mr Holmes wishes.'

She nodded and inclined her head to my friend graciously. 'Very well, Mr Sherlock Holmes, the future of Ruritania rests in your hands.'

Chapter Thirteen
The lodge at Lake Teufel

As the midnight hour approached, Holmes and I were back in our quarters in the royal palace discussing with Tarlenheim what our next move was to be. Queen Flavia had retired earlier, after expressing her gratitude to Holmes and requesting that Tarlenheim keep her fully informed of our decisions.

My heart went out to this lovely lady who was so isolated in her tragedy. The burden of title and duty weigh far heavier when personal sorrows invade the heart. It must seem to her, I mused, that the rock on which she had built her life and which had compensated for her lost love, Rassendyll, was rapidly crumbling away.

Holmes had asked for a map of Ruritania, which he pored over with his lens. This, and the other mysterious paraphernalia contained in his travelling bag, had been retrieved by one of Tarlenheim's men earlier that night from the livery stable where they had been left. Eventually Holmes's long finger pinpointed a spot on the map.

'I am convinced Rassendyll is being kept here,' he announced.

Tarlenheim examined the location.

'In Lake Teufel!' he remarked with astonishment.

'Not in the lake, my friend, but at the late King's fishing-lodge,' explained Holmes.

The Ruritanian looked doubtful. 'What leads you to this conclusion?'

'Several small details. Holstein, in his arrogant confidence, actually pointed the lodge out to us on our way to the Boar's Head, thinking we would not live long enough to use such information, even if we appreciated its significance. He told us that the lodge was now totally neglected, yet I clearly observed the morning sun glinting on the windows. Sunlight does not glint on neglected, grimy panes. There was also a small, shiny rowing boat tied up in the reeds just below the lodge. The ravages of time and weather would have sunk the boat or swept it away long ago, unless, of course, the boat is in use and the lodge tenanted. It is also true to say that Rupert, in utilising the fishing lodge for his own ends, is following his policy of taking over all the properties of the King not in current use.'

The change of expression on Tarlenheim's face as my friend spoke was most remarkable. His features shifted from disbelief to suppressed excitement.

'It is, of course, possible,' he conceded. 'The lodge is close enough to the Castle of Zenda to be of great convenience to Rupert. It is at least worth investigating in the morning. I'll take a body of men with me and search the place.'

'No!' exclaimed Holmes. 'That is the last thing you should do. We must go, the three of us alone, without being observed. We need to watch the lodge from a safe distance to ascertain what exactly is going on there.'

Tarlenheim wore a worried frown.

'Please trust me. The situation is too delicate to be solved by the use of force. It is cunning, nerve and caution which will aid us the best.'

'Will you not tell me what is in your mind? I do not like acting without knowing the reason.'

'All in good time. Please bear with me. My ideas are not, as yet, clearly formulated in my own mind and are, to some extent, dependent on the results of our reconnaissance. I will not keep you in the dark any longer than necessary, I assure you.'

'Very well,' replied Tarlenheim reluctantly.

'What time shall we start?'

'Well, as Watson and I have spent most of the day in a deep sleep, a few hours' rest should see us refreshed and ready to leave.'

'Very good. It is about an hour's ride to the lodge. We shall be able to arrive before sunrise.'

'Excellent. You are game, are you not, Watson?'

'Certainly,' I averred, 'but I would welcome some breakfast before we depart.'

Both men laughed.

'Of course, old fellow. I'm sure our friend, Tarlenheim, will be able to arrange something.'

'Something warm,' I prompted, remembering the cold meat and cheeses of my previous breakfast.

'While Rudolf Rassendyll was in the Palace he began each day with ham and eggs. How would that suit you, Dr Watson?' asked Tarlenheim.

'It would suit me very well,' I grinned.

* * *

Some time before dawn the following day, glowing warmly from the promised breakfast, we set off on horseback for Lake Teufel and the King's fishing lodge. It was a moonless night, with a few stars in the indigo heavens, and Holmes and I kept very close to Tarlenheim as he led the way. Shortly after leaving the city we plunged into the Forest of Zenda. In the dark no distinguishable path could be detected, but Tarlenheim manoeuvred his way through the thick foliage without hesitation. Soon the sky began to lighten and we were able to see the shimmer of grey water through the trees. We then came upon one of the largest oak trees I have ever seen, its massive branches reaching far out into the surrounding wood.

'That is the Elfberg Oak,' said Tarlenheim. 'The story goes that it was planted in the fifteenth century by Gustav, the first of the Elfberg monarchs. It is supposed to stand while ever there is an Elfberg on the throne of Ruritania.'

'It looks sturdy enough to repel even Rupert's challenge,' commented Holmes sardonically.

We had only just ridden past the great oak when Tarlenheim motioned us to stop. 'I think it would be wise to walk the remaining half mile or so,' he said, dismounting.

Holmes and I followed suit and tethered our horses in the heart of a thick clump of bushes, where they were quite hidden from view. We travelled down a beaten track a short distance, before Tarlenheim directed us to leave it to continue our journey cutting through the thick undergrowth. As we approached the fishing lodge from the rear, the land rose gradually. On reaching the brow of a gentle escarpment, we found ourselves looking down on the lodge some twelve feet below.

It was still and quiet, with no sign of life except, as Holmes pointed out, for wisps of grey smoke emerging from the chimney stack. 'Well, someone is in residence,' he whispered. 'Make yourselves comfortable: we may be in for a long wait.'

As events turned out there was great truth in Holmes's prophecy, but it was not long before we were able to witness some activity.

The orange sun was rising in the sky, just beginning to warm the air and disperse the hesitant morning mist billowing in from the lake, when we heard the front door of the lodge open; a man in dark breeches and a rough-woven collarless shirt stepped out, stretching himself. He had his back to us, but from his height, bearing and the thatch of dark red hair, it was apparent that this was Rudolf Rassendyll. I turned excitedly to Holmes who nodded casually in confirmation of my surmise.

Tarlenheim also showed signs of great excitement at our discovery. 'This is wonderful,' he hissed.

As Rassendyll turned, allowing us to see his face for the first time, I was able to note for myself his stunning likeness to Rudolf V. It is true that I had only seen photographs of the Ruritanian ruler, but to my eyes Rassendyll, even without the royal uniform, was a mirror image of the King.

Another figure emerged from the lodge, wearing the tunic of the Blues and carrying a rifle. He approached Rassendyll, uttering some words to him which we could not hear. As the two men engaged in conversation, the officer turned, allowing us a glimpse of his face. He was a middle-aged man with a broken nose and a sallow complexion.

'That is Captain Salberg, one of Rupert's most trusted officers,' whispered Tarlenheim.

The two men appeared to be at ease with one another and on friendly terms, but Salberg never relaxed his hold on his rifle. Together they wandered to the water's edge.

'I wonder how many more of Rupert's men are inside the lodge,' I queried.

'Only time will tell, but I suspect there will not be many, for this seems to be a relaxed kind of imprisonment. Rupert has little worry that Rassendyll will try to escape. The guards will be there to prevent him from being snatched away, rather than to stop him from breaking free,' observed Holmes.

Tarlenheim pulled his rifle forward and aimed it in the direction of Salberg.

'I could so easily pick him off,' he claimed, 'and then we could seize Rassendyll and make our escape.'

'Apart from rescuing Rassendyll from his enemies, that action would do nothing but harm to our cause,' replied Holmes.

Tarlenheim frowned, but lowered his rifle. 'I know you are right, sir, but the opportunity is so very tempting.'

As he was speaking another man appeared from the lodge wearing a white apron round his middle. He called to the other two and returned inside.

'It looks as if breakfast is served,' I said wistfully.

'Don't tell me you are hungry again, Doctor,' remarked Tarlenheim with what I took to be a twinkle in his eye.

'From what we have seen,' said Holmes, 'it would appear that there are only two men guarding Mr Rassendyll.'

'There may be others inside.'

'True, Watson. We shall have to wait and see.'

Nothing happened for the following couple of hours and then Rassendyll and Salberg emerged once more. The officer still carried his rifle, while Rassendyll was burdened with fishing tackle, which he dumped in a rowing boat tied up at the lakeside. Pulling the boat from the reeds both men clambered aboard. I realised this must be the boat that Holmes had spied from the coach on our journey to the Boar's Head. With Rassendyll manning the oars they set a course for the centre of the lake. By now the sun was well up, its reflection shimmering on the blue waters.

Sherlock Holmes stirred by my side. 'Somehow I've got to talk to Rassendyll alone without his captors knowing,' said he. 'I need to inform him of the situation as it now stands and include him in our plans.'

'How on earth are you going to manage that?' I asked.

'I shall have to gain entry to the lodge unseen and hide myself away in Rassendyll's room until I can speak to him in private.'

'What if Watson and I fire our guns some way back in the forest? Whoever is left in the lodge would be bound to leave it and invest-igate. The diversion would give you time enough to slip into the lodge unobserved.'

'Too risky. Suspicions would be aroused. It is imperative that they do not suspect a thing.'

'What then do you suggest?'

Before Holmes could reply to Tarlenheim's question we heard the sound of hooves in the distance. Gradually the sound grew louder and then, out of the forest into the clearing by the lodge, came a horseman dressed in the uniform of the Blues. He dismounted at some distance from the building and waited. Moments later the man we had seen earlier wearing the white apron reappeared, but now dressed in full uniform, and, after exchanging brief words with the newcomer, mounted the horse and rode back down the path into the forest.

'Obviously changing guards,' said I.

Holmes nodded. 'Yes. And this seems to confirm that there are only two of them. Now is the ideal time to act. While Salberg is out on the lake, if we can distract this new fellow long enough for me to gain entry to the lodge . . . '

As Holmes was saying this a worrying thought struck me. 'But how, eventually, will you escape?'

'I shall have Rassendyll to help me in that operation. It's the matter of distracting the guard without arousing his suspicions that is the real problem.'

'I have an idea,' I proclaimed, as a plan flashed into my mind. Eagerly I outlined the strategy to my two companions.

'Excellent, Watson,' said Holmes, smiling. 'Simple, but effective. I see no reason why we should not chance putting it into operation at once.'

Tarlenheim nodded his agreement. 'I will cover the good Doctor with my rifle,' he said, patting his weapon.

After some further brief refinements of the plan we set it in motion. Holmes, crouching low, moved swiftly to the stretch of woodland directly behind the lodge. After allowing him time to slip down the incline to the rear of the building I made my way back through the forest to where we had hidden the horses and then joined the main pathway.

Minutes later, with my heart pounding, I emerged from the trees into the clearing some yards from the fishing lodge. The spread of melancholy water rippled to the right of me and I could discern, far away from the shore, the silhouette of the small boat with its two occupants. I whistled loudly and merrily and, with as much nonchalance as I could muster, I approached the lodge. Before I had covered many yards the door burst open and the Blues officer rushed out with a rifle aimed in my direction.

'Halt! Do not come any further!' he cried as he confronted me.

I did as ordered with an air of casual puzzlement. 'Certainly, my good man,' I replied cheerily. 'Don't tell me I am trespassing? I was assured that I had the right of way through these woods.'

The man approached me cautiously and prodded me with his rifle. 'Who are you?' he barked.

'Hawkins is the name. Anthony Hawkins. English subject.' I gave a polite bow. 'I'm on a kind of walking holiday in your beautiful country. I've heard so much about the Forest of Zenda and the lake that I couldn't resist having a look for myself. I do hope I haven't broken any laws.'

The officer eyed me with doubt. While he did so I was able to detect some movement behind him at the far corner of the lodge. Holmes was making his move.

'Show me your papers.'

'I'm afraid I don't have them with me. To be honest, I really didn't think I would need them for a stroll in the woods. They are back at the inn with the rest of my luggage. Do you want to come back with me to inspect them?' I turned, as if to retrace my steps.

'Stop where you are!' he snapped angrily and I felt a cold shiver of fear as I heard the cocking of his rifle. It was then I realised that, although I was being covered, if this Blues' officer took it into his head to shoot me, it would be unlikely that Tarlenheim could retaliate before the deed was done. I turned and addressed the officer crossly.

'I say, I hope you don't intend to use that weapon on me. I'll have you know I have connections at the British Court. Her Royal Majesty Queen Victoria and her government would not take it lightly if I'm shot. And that, my good man, would certainly mean trouble for you.'

The Ruritanian frowned and, for a fleeting moment, there was a sign of uncertainty and concern in his gaze. It was then that I felt confident that I could successfully bluff my way out of the tricky situation I had manufactured for myself.

'Look here,' I continued in a more reasonable tone, 'if I've transgressed some law of property, it was done in all innocence, I assure you, and I apologise. I am quite prepared to pay a fine, but, mind you, if it's a large amount, you will have to accept English money. I have only a few Ruritanian marks on my person.'

There was a pregnant pause, during which he continued to eye me suspiciously, as he tried to make up his mind about this bizarre British intruder. His face reflected the uncertainty he felt about my tale, but I was relieved to see his finger relax on the trigger of the rifle. Eventually he spoke: 'Return the way you came, Englishman, and keep out of the forest in future. It is the Royal preserve.'

'Certainly,' I said with unctuous courtesy. 'Awfully sorry to have troubled you. I can assure you it will not happen again. Good day.' I smiled, tipped my hat and, with a warm sense of relief, I did as he commanded.

I walked for some distance back along the pathway, still adopting my carefree air, not daring to look back in case the man was tracking me. After I had gone two-thirds of a mile I surreptitiously checked that I was not being followed and then broke from the track, plunging once more into the deep undergrowth. As swiftly as I was able I made my way back to our hiding place, where Tarlenheim was still keeping vigil.

He greeted me with a broad grin. 'A fine performance, *Herr Doktor*. You had me totally convinced.'

I gave a smile and a nod of gratification. 'Did Holmes succeed?'

'Yes. He gained access to the lodge through a window at the rear.'

'Good,' I said with relief, settling down into the hiding place more comfortably. 'Now all we can do is wait.'

*   *   *

In the late afternoon Rassendyll and Salberg returned from the fishing trip, carrying several large carp as evidence of their success.

I began to grow concerned about Holmes and wondered whether he had been able to secrete himself safely in the lodge. At the back of my mind was the worrying possibility that Rassendyll was allowed no privacy in his captivity and that Holmes would thus have no opportunity to speak to him alone and, what was worse, would have no means of escape.

The sun began to set and the day to fade, but all Tarlenheim and I could do was remain where we were, waiting. Holmes could have been discovered and taken prisoner for all we knew. There was no knowing. Only time would tell.

As the stars began to prick the evening sky the air grew chill. I consulted my hunter, but it was getting too dark to see the figures clearly. In the encroaching darkness I felt the forest come alive with night creatures. There were strange rustlings and eerie cries, all contributing to a general unease calculated to set one's nerves on edge.

Eventually, the lights went out in the lodge and the smoke from the chimney died away. Despite the cold and the anxiety I felt, my eyes began to droop and I shifted stealthily in an attempt to keep myself awake and to relieve the stiffness my limbs felt after lying in one position for a long time.

'There is little point in watching the lodge now,' said Tarlenheim, pulling away from the edge of the escarpment. 'In this darkness it is impossible to see anything clearly.'

As I turned to agree with him, there came a more distinct rustling of grass behind us than I had heard previously. We both turned abruptly in the direction of the noise. Far off in the depths of the forest an owl screeched its night call, further tensing my nerves.

And then I saw, some little distance away from us in the darkness of the wood, the vague outline of a figure creeping towards us.

Chapter Fourteeen

Rassendyll

'Good evening, gentlemen. Sorry to have kept you waiting,' said a familiar voice.

'Holmes, by all that's wonderful. It's you,' I whispered hoarsely.

'Who were you expecting? Rupert of Hentzau?' Holmes chuckled gently.

'Your mission – it has been successful?' asked Tarlenheim.

'Indeed it has, but I suggest we retreat to warmer and more congenial surroundings before we discuss the matter further.'

Nearly two hours later we were back in our quarters at the Palace in Strelsau, settled before a blazing log fire. Tarlenheim and I were devouring bowls of appetising stew provided by one of the kitchen maids whom he had roused from her slumbers to attend on us. Gradually I began to feel the natural warmth and suppleness return to my limbs. Holmes sat by the grate, pipe in hand, giving us a résumé of his adventures.

'Despite its outward appearance, the fishing lodge is quite compact. There is a central sitting room where the meals are also taken. There are two bathrooms, a kitchen and four bedrooms, three of which were being used. When I entered through one of the back windows I had to decide quickly which of the bedrooms was occupied by Rassendyll. Despite your sterling work in distracting the guard – your resourcefulness never fails to astound me, old fellow – I still had precious little time to make my decisions. Luckily, I observed the hairbrush in the second room that I entered and saw several fine red hairs caught in the bristles. I was then left with the rather undignified expedient of concealing myself under the bed.

'And there I stayed for some considerable time. Rassendyll returned about five in the afternoon and spread out on the bed for a nap. When I was convinced he was alone and sure that he was sleeping, from the sound of his regular, heavy breathing, I determined to emerge from my hiding and make my presence known to him. I was just about to do so when the door opened and Salberg entered. He looked to be making a routine check on his captive for, seeing that Rassendyll was asleep, he retreated without disturbing him.

'After a few minutes' interval, I slid from under the bed and went to secure the door, but the lock had been removed, obviously as a precaution. Despite the apparently amicable relationship that Rassendyll had with his turnkeys, they did not trust him at all. I slipped a chair under the doorknob to act as a jam in case I was interrupted before I had carried out what I came to do. It would not prevent a forced entry, but it might allow me a fraction of time to conceal myself away again before the intruders broke in.

'As I secured the chair Rassendyll stirred. I rushed to the bed and clamped my hand over his mouth. His eyes sprang open in alarm. "I am a friend from England," I whispered urgently into his ear. "Please do not make a sound or we are both done for and Queen Flavia is doomed."

'His face registered shock and bewilderment, but he nodded his head in agreement and I felt his body relax a little. As swiftly and as briefly as I could I told him who I was and why I was there. I recounted Sapt's visit to Baker Street, his subsequent murder by Holstein, our rescue of Rassendyll's nephew and our encounter with Count Rupert. Finally, I told him of the death of the King.

'Understandably he was stunned by my revelations and I could see the conflicting emotions of despair and fury racking his thoughts. However, before he could reply coherently, we heard a noise in the corridor outside the room. Quickly, without a word, he sprang from the bed and rushed to remove the chair from jamming the door, while I slipped back under the bed. Rassendyll had only just swung the chair back to the dressing table where it belonged, when the door opened and Salberg entered.

' "Our evening meal will be ready soon, Mr Rassendyll, your Majesty. I beg you to join us at the table and then, after we've dined, I'd like another opportunity to thrash you at chess." Although he spoke in a casual, almost friendly fashion, there was a hard, sarcastic edge to his voice.

'Peering out from under the counterpane I could see that Rassendyll was pretending to examine some feature or mark on his face in the dressing table mirror. He turned briefly to Salberg and replied in a preoccupied manner. "I'll be with you shortly."

'Salberg grunted some response and left. At the sound of his retreating footsteps Rassendyll crouched down by my hiding-place.

"I must go now or it will look suspicious. After dinner I shall have to play this wretched fellow at chess. I'll let him win and pretend to have a headache and need an early night – then we can talk further."

'It was some considerable time later when Rassendyll returned and we were able to continue our conversation. In the meantime I occupied myself in that confined space by working out my proposed plan in close detail. On his return Rassendyll told me as much of Rupert's scheme as he knew. When the King of Bohemia arrives by rail at the border customs post on the day after tomorrow, he will be met by Hentzau and Rassendyll, posing as King Rudolf. Together they will board the Royal Train to greet the Bohemian monarch and, with him, journey to Strelsau, where it is expected that Queen Flavia will be waiting. Rupert must think that Rudolf is alive, but too "ill" for any public appearances.

'The crowd, on seeing Rassendyll emerge from the train in Strelsau, will accept him as the King and, in such public circumstances, Flavia, presented with this *fait accompli*, will have to follow suit. Thus Rupert will have made his first successful move towards securing the Crown for himself.'

Tarlenheim and I were struck dumb by the audacity of Rupert's plan and, before we could muster any coherent comment, Holmes had continued with his narrative.

'Of course, now that Rassendyll knew his nephew was in safe hands again, he was eager to throw his lot in with us and escape that very moment, until I pointed out the implications of such action; how his escape now would only further jeopardise the monarchy and Flavia's future. In great detail I explained my proposed plan of action to him and he agreed, without hesitation, to act under my instruction. All that then remained to be done was for him to distract the night guard with some complaint about cramp, while I crept out of the lodge by the way I came and rejoined you two.'

'Bravo!' exclaimed Tarlenheim, clapping my friend on the back, 'you have done exceptionally well.'

'Thank you,' said Holmes submissively.

'But now, my friend, you must explain to us the ramifications of your plan.'

Holmes readily concurred and, while we sat in rapt attention, he presented to us his daring and ingenious scheme designed to defeat Count Rupert of Hentzau and bring stability to the Ruritanian throne. After he had finished, there was a moment's silence and then Tarlenheim spoke.

'It is quite brilliant,' he said quietly, 'but also very dangerous. I must confess that I have grave doubts that it can be carried through successfully.'

'We have neither time nor resources to allow us the luxury of doubt,' Holmes remarked simply. 'Any plan, if it is to catch the enemy off guard, is, by its very nature, audacious, incorporating a marked element of risk. There is, I fear, no easier or more probable solution as far as my intellect apprehends the problem. Do you have any alternative idea?'

Our companion shook his head.

'Then we go ahead?' asked Holmes, casting a questioning glance at Tarlenheim, who clasped his hand in response.

'We go ahead,' he said resolutely.

'It is essential that we put the Queen clearly in the picture and ensure we have her blessing,' I pointed out.

'Quite right, Watson. She has a central role to play.'

'There will be an opportunity in the morning to discuss the matter with Her Majesty,' said Tarlenheim. 'Indeed, I should be obliged, gentlemen, if you would be so kind as to attend a brief ceremony at dawn.'

'The King's funeral?' queried Holmes.

'Yes. By the very nature of his death and the uncertainty of events, only a selected few have been informed of his passing and therefore his burial must be held in secret without the appropriate pomp and ceremony.' Tarlenheim looked sad and tired as he stared into the grate, shaking his head slowly. 'What a sorry state our country is in. Who knows what will happen to our monarchy and Queen Flavia?'

Holmes placed his hand reassuringly on the Ruritanian's shoulder. 'Bear up, Tarlenheim,' said he. 'Be of stout heart. The next forty-eight hours will be crucial and we shall need your best efforts.'

*   *   *

For the second night in a row we were granted only a few hours' sleep and, for me, those were fretful. My mind was filled with so many thoughts, hopes and fears that, tired as I was, sleep refused to come. It seemed that I had only just fallen into an uneasy slumber when I was roused by Holmes to attend the King's burial.

The day had dawned cool and misty with a thin drizzle hanging in the air, a fitting backdrop for such a sombre occasion. We gathered for the ceremony in a small, enclosed garden within the Palace grounds. There were only six mourners: the Queen, pale and tranquil of feature; the doctor who had attended the King during his last illness; the Archbishop of Strelsau, who officiated; Fritz von Tarlenheim; Sherlock Holmes and myself.

As the simple coffin was lowered into the ground Flavia cast a red rose down on to the casket. 'If only, Rudolf . . . if only . . . ' she breathed softly to herself. Her eyes were dry, but they reflected a deep and inexpressible regret.

There was a dark mood of gloom about us, far stronger than the air of bereavement that pervades any funeral. It was, I thought, generated by the grim realisation of the essential wrongness of burying the country's king in this brief and unceremonious manner. It was a dispiriting experience.

Tarlenheim and the doctor filled in the unmarked grave with loose earth as the Archbishop intoned some prayers over it. Holmes's face was stern and immobile and even I, who knew him so well, was unable to determine what thoughts were to be found behind his impassive mask.

We stood for some moments in silent respect and then returned to the Palace, where, after formal expressions of condolence were expressed, Tarlenheim, Holmes and I were invited into the Queen's chamber. There we were given warming glasses of brandy with which to pledge a final toast to the dead King. After a brief period of reflection, we fell to discussing our immediate future. Apparently, Tarlenheim had already briefed the Queen on the previous day's events at the fishing lodge and she now asked Holmes to explain his strategy to her.

As Queen Flavia sat, still and serene, Holmes paced before the large marble fireplace explaining the details of his proposed action in his quiet methodical way.

'You have an audacious mind, Mr Holmes,' the Queen remarked when my friend had finished speaking. Pausing briefly, she looked directly at him, her eyes closely examining his face. 'You know, I believe you can do it!'

'Thank you, ma'am,' he returned humbly.

'And now, tell me, how is Rudolf? Did he seem well?'

'He appeared in the best of health.'

'And he, too, has readily fallen in with your scheme?'

Holmes gave a nod of assurance.

'He would,' said the Queen, allowing herself the briefest of smiles, which nonetheless lit up her pallid features, reminding one what a beautiful women she was. 'Gentlemen,' she said, 'recharge your glasses for another toast. To the success of Sherlock Holmes and the downfall of Count Rupert of Hentzau!'

Chapter Fifteen
Rupert again

We had only the remainder of that day in which to prepare ourselves against the arrival of King Wilhelm of Bohemia. Tarlenheim was necessarily absent, visiting the cavalry garrison on the other side of the city in order to give final instructions for the royal occasion which, to all but a few, would be regarded as a normal visit from a friendly Head of State. Struggling against the language barrier in the morning newspaper, it was apparent that the exciting element of this event for the population of Ruritania in general and Strelsau in particular was the possible re-emergence of their sovereign from his lengthy convalescence.

Holmes and I, left on our own, kept within the confines of the Palace. My friend was broody and uncommunicative and I was left to my own thoughts, which I confess were filled with misgivings, uncertainties and fears. I could only wonder what Count Rupert's reactions had been to the news of the deaths of Holstein and Sir Roger and to the escape of Holmes and myself. Was he now plotting revenge? Or was his ambition too preoccupied with thoughts of tomorrow for him to bother about two foreign interlopers. I hoped that he was so supremely confident of success that he did not view our escape as a real threat, believing he could deal with us, if necessary, after assuming power.

Early in the afternoon, I was dozing in my chair while Holmes experimented with his make-up kit. Suddenly I was roused by a knock at the door. Queen Flavia entered, her face clouded with anxiety.

'Mr Holmes! He is here at the Palace!' she urgently whispered.

'Rupert?' my friend asked incredulously.

'Yes. He has requested an audience.'

'By all that's holy! The audacity of the man!'

'What shall I do? Fritz has not yet returned and I am unsure of what action to take.'

There was only a brief pause before my friend replied. 'You must see him, of course. Watson and I will attend on you, with your permission.'

'Yes, of course,' she agreed with some relief.

Without further discussion we accompanied the Queen to the King's reception room, which was dominated by a life-size portrait of Rudolf, painted shortly after the Coronation. He seemed to stare down with interest at our entrance. Below the portrait stood a pair of gilt thrones on a dais. Flavia seated herself here, while Holmes and I placed ourselves on either side of the thrones.

'Why don't we grab him now, while we have the chance?' I whispered to my friend.

'If only it were that simple, Watson. Remember that, although Rupert is the dominant force behind the Blues, he is only the leader. There are others ready to take his place, as passionate as he to see the downfall of the Elfbergs. To rid Ruritania of this threat, the Blues need to be discredited publicly and then weeded out, root and branch.'

Before I was able to respond, Rupert of Hentzau was admitted to the chamber. He strode to the dais with a confident swagger, a supercilious grin on his face, which hardened rather than softened his cold features. He knelt before the Queen and kissed her hand, but his actions were performed in such a manner as to have an air of sarcastic mockery.

'Your Majesty, I thank you for granting me an audience,' he said smoothly. 'I am pleased to see you in such good health and in such interesting company.' He eyed Holmes and me, smiling. 'The last time I saw these gentlemen I feared for their lives. As a matter of fact, I still do.'

'Count Rupert,' Queen Flavia said with cool authority, 'my time is precious and I have none of it to spare for such comment. Please come to the point of your visit. I have no joy in this interview.'

There was such a spark of courage and defiance in the Queen's words that my heart swelled in admiration of her.

Rupert boldly looked around the room in mock scrutiny. 'His Majesty is still – indisposed, I gather?' On receiving no answer to his taunt, he continued. 'No matter. My words will serve their purpose equally, addressed to you. Now, if I am to come directly to the heart of the matter, it is essential that we drop all pretence. We are both fully aware that Rudolf is incapable of putting in an appearance tomorrow to greet the King of Bohemia – unless, of course, you are determined to place his gibbering Majesty on show to his subjects.'

It took great restraint on my part to prevent me from stepping forward and striking this arrogant villain for this cruel and vicious statement. The Queen, however, remained icily silent, although I saw her knuckles whiten as she clasped the arms of her throne.

'Why not take the easy way out, Flavia?' continued Rupert, who was by now completely relaxed and obviously enjoying himself. 'I can supply you with another King – the very same who was crowned in Strelsau Cathedral just three years ago. A man with whom –' he hesitated in a theatrical fashion before going on – with whom, shall we say, you share certain passions.'

Flavia hooded her eyes in a piercing stare, but made no comment.

'I offer you a dignified solution to your dilemma. The country will see their king restored to them again – and you will be united with the man you love.'

'What an altruist you are,' remarked Holmes, matching Hentzau's earlier sarcasm.

Rupert beamed at Holmes. 'Well, not quite, Mr Sherlock Holmes. There are certain advantages for me also.'

'Count Rupert,' said the Queen in a voice devoid of any emotion, 'you are wasting your words and my time. King Rudolf will be in attendance tomorrow to greet his Highness King Wilhelm. But I tell you this to spare you from further pursuit of this matter: I would rather die than aid you to get your greedy and unwholesome clutches on the Crown. This audience is at an end.'

'Very well. You have made your choice clear. I admire your bravado, but today's empty words will be blown away by the winds of tomorrow.'

As he turned to depart, Rupert of Hentzau returned his attention to Holmes, a sneer still on his face. 'You have boxed yourself into a corner this time, Englishman. One from which you will not escape. The grains of sand are running out for you: soon I shall control all the forces in this country and there will be nowhere to hide. Then, I assure you, I shall grant you no mercy.'

His mockery had all vanished now and Rupert spoke with cold and vicious anger. Holmes looked genuinely worried and lost for words, his brows contracting with concern. Satisfied at the effect his threats had made on my friend, he turned once more towards the Queen for a parting shot.

'Your Majesty,' and he bowed low. 'I will see you at the railway station tomorrow morning.'

With that he turned on his heel to stride swiftly from the chamber, leaving us temporarily numbed into silence. Then Sherlock Holmes burst into laughter; both Flavia and I looked at him in bewilderment.

'My apologies,' he spluttered, when eventually his amusement had subsided. 'Arrogance in one so essentially vulnerable always provokes me to laughter.'

'Vulnerable?' I echoed my friend in surprise at his description of the confident Rupert of Hentzau.

'In truth, my friend. Rupert's coming here was audacious, I grant you, but it is also an indication that we have somewhat shaken his certainty. My apparent distress at his personal threat was performed in order to bolster further his belief that we can, in no way, successfully oppose him.'

'You had me confused, Mr Holmes,' admitted the Queen, 'I thought you were losing your nerve.'

'Let us hope that I continue to be successful in all my deceptions,' Holmes replied earnestly.

* * *

I spent most of the rest of the day on my own. On Tarlenheim's return to the Palace, he and Holmes spent some time together, discussing military operations organised for the following day. My friend then shut himself away in his bedroom to carry out some experiments in private. Thrown on my own devices, I let my thoughts dwell on the dramatic events of the past few days, clarifying the intricate details of the case as I did so. When I had arranged the train of events clearly in my mind, I began to write up some notes regarding the Hentzau Affair (as I had come to think of it). I realised as I wrote that, because of the highly confidential and politically dangerous nature of the investigation, publication of my account would not be possible for decades – if at all. I just hoped that it would have a satisfactory conclusion.

That evening Tarlenheim, Holmes and I dined with the Queen in her private room. It was a subdued occasion, for we were all lost in our own thoughts and were reluctant to share them. However, when the meal was over and we sat back with our brandies, Tarlenheim gave us a full description of the various plans for the morrow, including the deployment of the King's forces for the arrival of King Wilhelm of Bohemia. His Royal Train was due into the Strelsau terminus at noon. Stepping out on to the red carpet, he would be greeted by Queen Flavia. The two were then to travel by state coach to the Palace where a banquet in honour of the visiting monarch was due to take place.

'However, as we now know,' Holmes commented, 'Rupert intends to intercept the train at the border post with Rassendyll, so that when it arrives in Strelsau, King Wilhelm will emerge alongside "King Rudolf". This and our own little set of surprises should make for an interesting day. No matter how meticulously we have planned, we must be ready for all contingencies.'

It seemed strange and unreal to me to consider the vast numbers of people who were to be engaged in the proposed festivities: the Ruritanian nobility, the various foreign ambassadors (with one notable exception), the military and an army of servants, all of whom, as far as we knew, were ignorant of the dramatic undercurrents and the crucial drama which was to be acted out.

At the end of the evening Holmes requested some private moments with the Queen, and so Tarlenheim and I left them alone together. I retired to my room, exhausted, but with the knowledge that I would sleep little. I felt those strangely compatible emotions of apprehension and excitement coursing through my veins. As I lay there in the dark, watching the moonlit clouds drift past my window, I knew that whatever tomorrow might bring, it presented Sherlock Holmes with the greatest challenge of his career.

Chapter Sixteen
The forest of Zenda

As luck would have it, the next day dawned grey and overcast, with storm clouds rolling across a leaden sky. I had slept fitfully and was glad to drag myself from my bed to get dressed. I did not know if it was the gloomy weather or my own nervous apprehensions about the day's events that dampened my spirits, but I felt quite low when I knocked on Holmes's door. All black thoughts were immediately chased from my mind on entering, for there, sitting at the dressing table in a magnificent white uniform, complete with gold-fringed epaulettes and a crimson sash, was His Majesty King Rudolf V of Ruritania! He turned at my entrance and smiled a greeting.

'Will I do, old fellow?' came the familiar voice.

Holmes's capacity for disguise was a constant source of amazement and surprise over the years. I well remember with what startling effect he confronted me, in my own house, in the character of an old bibliophile. It was on that occasion that, for the first and last time in my life, I fainted. I recall also how cleverly he fooled me with his disguise of a venerable Italian priest when we were fleeing from the clutches of Professor Moriarty and his gang. Here, then was a refinement of that remarkable skill. Holmes had not merely adopted a disguise, he had become the very image of another person.

'It is wonderful,' I gasped.

'Well, I think it will suffice. This has been my main aid,' explained he, pulling a cloth from the Coronation portrait of King Rudolf which was now leaning against his wall. 'The Queen had it moved here at my request and I have been working on my appearance all night. The colour of the hair presented the greatest challenge. Fortunately I was able to obtain a cutting before the King was buried in order to match it exactly. At first I thought I would be able to dye my own, but the process proved to be too long-winded and imprecise and there was also the added complication of matching the texture. My hair is too fine to simulate the thickness of Rudolf's growth. Therefore, I resorted to tinting a suitable wig: this is my third attempt.'

He gestured towards the two discarded failures lying on the table, which was also littered with various chemicals, bowls of dye and hair clippings.

'Once the hair was prepared,' he continued, 'I began to work on the face. The shape and length of the nose was the most difficult feature to reproduce, but with a discreet use of putty and shading down the side, I believe I've managed a tolerable transformation.'

He stood up, brushing down the uniform with his hands, and then examined the full effect in a long mirror. 'The Queen approves. In fact, she was somewhat taken aback,' Holmes preened himself.

'I am not surprised,' said I.

'It is the voice which may be the real problem. As you must understand, I have studied photographs of the King and discussed his mannerisms with the Queen and Tarlenheim, but, never having heard Rudolf talk, recreating the actual timbre and resonance of his voice is difficult.'

'What of Rassendyll? His voice must be similar.'

'Yes, a close approximation. But making an approximation of an approximation, there is bound to be a weakness in its authenticity. I think it safer to adopt a slightly hoarse tone, like this.' He demonstrated. 'A King who has been ill for some time is likely to have a weakened voice.'

'That is true,' I admitted, 'but will it fool Hentzau?'

'We shall soon see, old friend.'

'King Rudolf' pulled on his gloves and regarded me with that glint of excitement in his eyes. 'Are you ready, Watson? The game is afoot.'

* * *

We made our farewells to the Queen, and then Tarlenheim, who also was startled by the effectiveness of my friend's disguise, led us to the stables to collect our horses and the grisly cargo we needed to take with us. This was covered in sacking hanging limply over a third horse. Without words, we shook hands with Tarlenheim and set off once more for the Forest of Zenda, Holmes wearing a hooded riding cloak to hide his appearance.

On entering the dense wood, we headed for the large Elfberg Oak. Tethering our horses under cover nearby, we made our preparations.

Holmes cut loose the heavy bundle from the riderless horse and pulled away the sacking to reveal the corpse of an old man dressed in beggar's clothes.

'Tarlenheim assures me it is less than twelve hours old; one of the kitchen staff at the Palace who died of pneumonia yesterday.' He gave a grim smile. 'This old fellow will go on serving his country even after his death. Give me a hand, please, Watson.'

Together we carried the corpse and laid it across the pathway at a narrow stretch where trees already restricted the passage.

'Examination will show nothing more than a dead beggar,' said Holmes. 'Let us hope it gives us the few moments of diversion that we need.'

We retreated behind the Elfberg Oak to wait. By now a thin drizzle was falling, but, sheltered under the great tree, we remained dry.

It was some time after ten when we heard the sound of approaching riders. I clutched my revolver, my heart thumping against my ribs. In the distance, down the path, I could make out through the thin curtain of rain, a moving shimmer of blue. Gradually I was able to focus on the group of riders. It was the party we had been expecting. Holmes strained forward to gauge the number of horsemen, his features taut and exultant.

There were just four riders. In front were the two men on whom the future of Ruritania pivoted; slightly in the lead was the jaunty figure of Count Rupert of Hentzau, closely followed by Rudolf Rassendyll, who wore, like Holmes, the King's state uniform with a rain cape at his shoulders. They were followed by two Blues' officers, one of whom I recognised as Captain Salberg.

As they neared the figure on the pathway, Hentzau held up his hand, halting the others. Salberg and the Count dismounted, with Salberg going forward to inspect the obstruction. While this was happening, Rassendyll's horse appeared to shy, rearing up on its back legs, pawing the air violently, almost throwing its rider to the ground. Rassendyll gave a cry of alarm and threw his left arm back in a wild panic, hitting the mounted Blues officer in the face, the force of the blow being such that the soldier lost his balance and tumbled to the ground. Rassendyll's mount seemed to have a will of its own and, while he wrestled desperately with its reins, it bounded off the pathway at a tangent, into the thick undergrowth. With bellows of protest from Rassendyll, both horse and rider were swallowed up by the dark wood.

Rupert, who had by this time been informed that the figure on the ground was 'just some old ragamuffin', barked a series of commands as he raced back to his mount. The other two officers furiously scrambled into their saddles – but by now there was no sign of Rassendyll.

During the confusion, their charge emerged from the thick foliage by our side. Without one word being spoken, Holmes and Rassendyll quickly exchanged capes and then, taking the reins of Rassendyll's horse, my friend vaulted into the saddle and galloped away.

Rassendyll and I crouched low, peering round the tree's girth to watch the Blues in disarray, making sorties from the path into the wood in frantic search for the impostor King. And then the 'King' appeared, as if by magic, out of the trees to rejoin them. He gave all the signs of finally having gained control of his horse after a struggle, appearing unnerved and distraught.

Rupert, his face dark with anger, rode up and berated him furi-ously. Holmes replied earnestly, still seeming to be shaking from his ordeal, no doubt explaining how his horse had, for some reason, taken fright and how he had momentarily lost control. I watched the Count's face closely. He seemed completely unaware that he was addressing Sherlock Holmes and not Rudolf Rassendyll. His anger, it was clear, was directed at his prisoner's incompetent horsemanship and its resulting confusion. It looked as though the switch of impostor kings had succeeded and that the first stage of Holmes's plan had worked effectively. However, I was too old a hand at playing dangerous games with my friend to relax. I realised that this was but the first step on a dangerous and difficult journey and there were many more twists and turns to negotiate before we reached our goal.

The horsemen reformed themselves at Rupert's command and within moments they resumed their journey. As they passed close by me I saw Rupert's face still flushed with anger, while Holmes was suitably subdued. It was not long before the riders merged into the foliage on their way to the Border Customs Post where they would meet the Royal Train of the Bohemian King.

After they had disappeared from sight Rassendyll turned to me and grasped my hand warmly. 'You must be Watson, I take it,' he said.

I smiled and nodded

'Your friend is a clever and courageous man. His likeness to the King is remarkable.'

'I found myself smiling and nodding more. 'As is yours,' I pointed out.

Rassendyll gave a little chuckle. 'Well, Watson, I am in your hands now. What is the next move?'

'First cover yourself with this cloak and then we ride for the Palace.'

*   *   *

We entered the Palace by the rear gate and were met by an anxious Tarlenheim. His worried frown dissipated at the sight of Rassendyll and, on hearing of the success of our venture, his face lit up with pleasure and relief. He and Rassendyll hugged each other like long-lost brothers.

'I always said you were the bravest Elfberg of them all,' announced the Ruritanian.

'Or the unluckiest,' answered Rassendyll.

'Come, friend Rudolf, let us tell the Queen our good news. I know she is waiting anxiously to see you.'

If Tarlenheim's reunion with Rudolf had been emotional, it was nothing to that of the Queen's. It was not that they behaved in a physically demonstrative way, but, as they stood facing each other, the atmosphere was charged with emotion. It did not need the deductive powers of a Sherlock Holmes to see that the two were very much in love.

Rassendyll went on one knee and kissed the Queen's hand. 'Your Majesty, your humble servant is at your command,' he said softly.

Flavia's eyes moistened as she laid her hand on Rassendyll's head and gently smoothed back his hair. It was at this point that Tarlenheim and I made our discreet exit.

As we waited my mind returned to Sherlock Holmes. I wondered if everything was still running smoothly for him. I glanced at my watch and calculated that it would not be long before he reached the Customs Post. Fortunately there was little time for me to speculate on the possible hazards he could encounter, for it was soon time to prepare for the royal procession to the Central Station.

Shortly before noon, accompanied by a troop of the King's Cavalry, the Royal Coach, containing Rassendyll and the Queen, left the Palace. Tarlenheim and I, dressed in the uniforms of high-ranking officers, rode by the State Coach as it made its way through the mediaeval streets of Strelsau.

It was no longer raining and the city was thronged with cheering crowds eager to catch a glimpse of the King. People hung out of upstairs windows waving the green and gold-lozenged flag of Ruritania and shouting jubilantly as the coach passed by. It was moving to hear their cries of joy and love as the people saw their monarch apparently fully recovered and hearty.

As the procession turned into König Square, the great Ionic columns of the Central Station loomed into view and, as we neared the railway terminus, I felt my body stiffen with apprehension and fear. I knew that very soon we would reach the climax of this dangerous affair.

Chapter Seventeen
The Royal Train

I was not witness to the events I have recorded in the following chapter, but learned the details later. I now present them in a dramatised form in order to maintain a coherent narrative.

* * *

Despite the apparent ease with which Sherlock Holmes had managed to change places with Rudolf Rassendyll in the Forest of Zenda he knew that, due to the dim light in the forest and the drama of the moment, it had been comparatively easy to be accepted as Rassendyll at first. The real test would come later.

As the party of riders, led by Rupert of Hentzau, left the confines of the forest and started cantering down the highway towards the border they were approached by a squad of the King's soldiers. A Commander, whom Holmes had glimpsed in the Palace grounds the previous day, rode forward to meet them. As he did so, Holmes felt the hard prod of a pistol in his back.

'Play your part, Rassendyll, or you will not live to see Flavia again.' The whispered injunction came from Salberg, who had sidled close to him.

'What authority brings you here?' challenged the Commander, addressing Rupert.

Holmes let the rain cape slip away from his uniform and raised his head. 'Mine,' he said.

The Commander's jaw dropped. 'Your Majesty, I had no idea . . . ' he stammered, completely taken aback. Quickly pulling himself together, he saluted the 'King'.

Holmes smiled indulgently. 'That is quite all right, Commander. I am pleased to see you being so vigilant. There has been a slight change in my arrangements. I have decided to meet the King of Bohemia at Steinbach instead of in Strelsau and Count Rupert has been kind enough to accompany me.'

At this mention of Rupert, a puzzled look crossed the Commander's features, but he was experienced enough to know not to make any comment on this unlikely alliance. 'It would be best, perhaps,' he suggested, 'if I led Your Majesty to the border, as my men are not expecting any official visitors.'

Holmes cast a glance at Rupert who gave him an almost imperceptible nod.

'Very well, Commander,' replied Holmes. 'The Count and I will follow you.'

The soldier saluted and, pulling his horse around, he led the way to the wooden Customs House, leaving Captain Salberg and the other Blues officer behind. At the building the Commander dismounted and headed up the steps before turning to address Holmes. 'If you would be so good as to wait here, Your Majesty, I will make arrangements for you,' he said, hardly waiting for acknowledgement before disappearing through the door.

Holmes and Count Rupert dismounted and tethered their horses while waiting. 'Remember, Englishman,' murmured Hentzau threateningly, 'one wrong move and you are a dead man.'

'There will be no wrong moves; I am resigned to my fate,' replied Holmes softly, averting his head from Rupert's gaze, not giving him the opportunity to study his features too closely.

A smile flashed across Rupert's face. 'You are being most sensible. Remember, that when we board the train you will introduce me to King Wilhelm as your close friend and adviser, and at no time will you suggest that I leave your side.'

Holmes gave a brief nod. 'That is understood.'

The Commander returned and ushered them into the Customs House, where six soldiers stood to attention as they passed through and out on to the railway station platform. Here two border guards were engaged in laying out a red runner for the royal visitor. The old guard, who had checked Holmes's papers a few days earlier, on seeing his King, approached him hesitantly.

'Your Majesty,' he said, bowing deeply. 'I was not informed that you were to be in attendance. I would have made arrangements to receive you properly, had I known.'

'I want no ceremony. There will be more than enough later,' replied Holmes curtly.

'As you wish, sire.' The time-weathered face cracked into an uneasy smile, adding to the general nervousness of the old man's demeanour. 'It is good to see you looking so well, Your Majesty.

We have not had the pleasure of your presence in these parts since the Royal Boar Hunt last spring.'

Holmes inclined his head and the old guard moved away to attend to his duties. However, before he was able to do so he was approached by the Commander who engaged him in a brief conversation.

The thin drizzle had stopped and, as the sky lightened, small patches of blue could be discerned breaking through. In the distance Holmes saw a pale grey banner of steam moving steadily towards them. It was not long before the locomotive came into view, prompting a flurry of activity on the platform. A guard of honour lined up on either side of Count Rupert and Holmes, who now stood on the red carpet in readiness to greet the Bohemian King when the train arrived.

The locomotive thundered in and hissed to a halt. When the great rolling clouds of steam had dispersed from the platform the royal carriage door opened. Out stepped Wilhelm Gottsreich Sigismond von Ormstein, King of Bohemia.

It may be remembered that Sherlock Holmes had encountered the Bohemian monarch a few years earlier when the King had enlisted the detective's services to retrieve a compromising photograph from his former mistress. This lady, the incomparable Irene Adler, had left an indelible impression on Holmes; for him she is always *the* woman: the events are recorded in *A Scandal in Bohemia*.

Holmes knew full well that he stood in grave danger of being recognised by King Wilhelm. However, it was some seven years since the two had met and the King had struck Holmes as having that streak of arrogance possessed by some powerful men which makes them fail to notice in any particular the features of others whom they regard as being on a lower social plane.

The two men moved forward to greet each other.

'What a pleasure and surprise to see you here, Rudolf. I had heard rumours of illness, but here you are, fresh of face.'

'It is always wise to distrust rumours, especially about a King. You should know that yourself. I remember in the past some talk of you and a certain American lady.'

Wilhelm laughed. 'True, true. We are the targets for mischievous talk. But tell me, where is the beautiful Flavia?'

'She is to greet us in Strelsau.'

'Good. Of course, Rudolf, you realise that the real reason for my visit is to see her. I insist she reserves all her dances for me.' He laughed heartily again, his large frame shaking with amusement.

Holmes returned a polite smile.

King Wilhelm cast a curious glance at Rupert.

'Allow me to introduce to you one of my young noblemen. This is Count Rupert of Hentzau, my close adviser and confidant.'

Rupert stepped forward and gave a curt bow.

'Good day, Count.'

'Your Highness,' replied Rupert in obsequious fashion.

'Well, gentlemen, do come aboard. Let us partake of some refreshment before we reach the capital.'

The three men boarded the train and, passing by two Bohemian halbardiers, entered a most luxuriously appointed compartment with mahogany-panelled walls, velvet drapes and rich Indian carpets. Here Holmes and Rupert were introduced to Boris Glasanov, the Bohemian Minister of Foreign Affairs, a tall, balding man in a frock coat.

'Be seated, gentlemen, and relax,' said King Wilhelm gaily, throwing himself down in a vast armchair. He rang a little bell and a servant appeared instantly and served drinks from a cabinet in the compartment.

Rupert did not stray from Holmes's side, while always giving the appearance of being attentive and subservient.

With a sudden jolt and a loud clanking of couplings the Royal Train pulled away from the border post.

'How long is our journey to Strelsau?' asked King Wilhelm.

'About an hour,' volunteered Rupert.

'Ah,' cried the Bohemian monarch, beaming. 'Time for a game of cards. What do you say, gentlemen?'

It was a rhetorical question and a card table was quickly set up and, in minutes, King Wilhelm was dealing.

Holmes was satisfied with this turn of events, as it prevented any serious discussion of royal affairs and of topics beyond his knowledge. He realised that, as long as he allowed the King of Bohemia to win his hand, the King would be happy enough to continue playing until the train reached its destination.

After some fifteen minutes of play the Captain of the Bohemian guard entered. King Wilhelm looked up at him with some annoyance. 'What is it?' he snapped.

'Your Majesty. The Commander in charge of the Ruritanian forces at the border is on the train and urgently requests a private audience with King Rudolf,' replied the guard in hushed tones.

'Damn it, we are in the middle of a hand.'

While secretly Holmes was puzzled by this development, outwardly he appeared quite nonchalant. 'Surely the matter can.wait until later,' he said languidly.

'The Commander insisted that it was urgent, sire,' came the reply.

'Oh, very well, I will see him. If you will excuse me for a moment, Wilhelm?'

Holmes rose to leave the compartment and, as he did so, Rupert motioned to do likewise.

'Oh, no, you don't,' said Wilhelm gruffly, but in good humour. 'We're not losing a second player. You can handle your Commander on your own, I'm sure, Rudolf.'

Rupert hesitated. He was in a cleft stick and he glowered at Holmes, who contrived to take no notice.

'Off you go, Rudolf, and hurry back,' ordered King Wilhelm, eager to continue the game.

Holmes left the compartment and followed the Bohemian officer down the corridor to the next coach.

'The Commander is waiting for you in there, sire,' he said, leaving Holmes to return to his own post.

Holmes entered the compartment indicated and, as he did so, he was momentarily aware that the blinds had been drawn just as the door was slammed shut behind him, plunging him into darkness. He turned rapidly to reach for the handle, but, before he was able to do so, someone grabbed him from behind. An arm held him round the neck and he felt the sharp point of a knife at his throat.

'All right,' came a voice out of the blackness, 'who are you? You are not King Rudolf, that is for sure. Speak quickly before I kill you.'

*   *   *

The situation in which Sherlock Holmes now found himself, held firmly by an unknown assailant, while a sharp blade hovered inches away from his jugular vein, was one that took him completely by surprise. Thorough as he had been in his planning, carefully considering the possible hazards that could arise during the course of his impersonation of King Rudolf, this eventuality had never once been contemplated.

'Who are you?' repeated the voice, which Holmes now recognised as belonging to the Commander who had escorted them to the railway station.

'I assure you I am a friend of your master,' croaked the detective, realising that there was no point in trying to claim that his assailant was mistaken and that he really was the King. 'By attacking me you are placing the Elfberg monarchy at grave risk.'

'If you continue to talk nonsense and refuse to tell the truth, I shall waste no further time on you.' The blade scraped the flesh of Holmes's throat.

The detective realised that whatever explanation he gave it would not convince the loyal officer of his veracity. Force rather than reason was the only means by which he could extricate himself from his awkward predicament. By now Holmes' eyes had become accustomed to the gloom. There were thin strips of light filtering into the carriage down the edges of the window blind that allowed him to determine a vague geography of the compartment. In what had first seemed pitch blackness he could now make out the shape and stance of his adversary.

'My papers are inside my tunic,' said Holmes desperately. 'They will give you proof of my identity and my mission.'

There was a moment's pause and then the Commander loosened his hold slightly, as he made to extract the documents from Holmes' tunic. The hold was still firm, but, because it had been relaxed and his assailant's attention had been temporarily distracted from the knife, Holmes was presented with the opportunity he needed.

I have recorded elsewhere references to my friend's fitness and agility in unarmed combat. He had studied Baritsu, a Japanese form of self-defence, based on weight and balance. Using these refined techniques, he inhaled deeply, pivoted on his heels and, dropping at the same time to a crouching position, was able to throw the Commander over his shoulder, where he landed sprawled on his back.

Holmes then leapt forward and released one of the window blinds. As it shot up with a staccato volley the compartment flooded with light.

The Commander was just about to rise to his feet when Holmes's foot flashed through the air, catching the hand which held the knife. The weapon flew upwards from the Commander's grasp, and Holmes snatched it by the handle. The Commander, dazed by the speed with which Holmes had turned the tables on him, was further surprised to see his attacker proffer a hand to pull him to his feet.

'I admit that I am not the King,' Holmes said to the bewildered officer in an urgent whisper, 'but I am impersonating him by royal command. There is a threat to the monarchy in which Count Rupert of Hentzau is inextricably involved. It is essential that I carry out the impersonation to foil this plot and ensure the safety of the Elfberg dynasty.'

Puzzlement and uncertainty clouded the Commander's face.

Holmes continued. 'I cannot answer any of the questions which are obviously racing through your mind at this moment. I can only ask you to trust me. If I really were an enemy, I could have killed you quite easily, rather than attempt an explanation.'

The Commander acknowledged this truth. 'But what of Count Rupert?'

'He does not know who I am and he must not know.' Holmes spoke with such earnest conviction that the Commander seemed finally to accept his story.

'Very well. I will say nothing.'

'You will not regret it,' Holmes assured him. 'However, before I return to the others, tell me how you knew I was not King Rudolf.'

'Your friendliness towards Count Rupert first put me on my guard. I spent some time with the King in the early spring of this year on a boar hunt and he became somewhat friendly towards me and confided his fear and hatred of Hentzau. From what he said to me on that occasion, I could hardly see him treating the Count as a close companion.

'Also, when I encountered you in the Forest of Zenda, you showed no apparent recognition of me. It was as though we had never met before. The old guard at the Customs House conveyed a similar impression to me. I felt sure you were an impostor.'

Holmes smiled. He was pleased that, at least, it was not his disguise that had given him away. 'A contingency I did not expect. However, you are to be complimented on your diligence and loyalty, Commander. I will see to it that, when this affair is over, the King shall hear of your actions.'

'That is not necessary. I want no benefit. The safety of the King will be reward enough.'

Holmes gave an understanding nod. 'And in pursuit of that goal I must now return to King Wilhelm's compartment and act as though nothing has happened and you must act similarly.'

'As you wish.'

'I will say that you wanted to see me in order to confirm the security arrangements for King Wilhelm's journey from the railway terminus to the Palace.'

The Commander opened the door for Holmes to leave. 'Good luck,' he said.

Moments later, Sherlock Holmes entered the royal compartment. The Bohemian monarch looked up rather petulantly as he resumed his seat by the card table. 'I'm glad you're back, Rudolf. Now perhaps my luck will change. At the moment, Count Rupert seems to be holding all the best cards.'

Chapter Eighteen
The reception

While we waited for the Royal Train to arrive my stomach was aching with nerves. It was only with the greatest effort that I managed to show a placid exterior.

Queen Flavia and Rassendyll stood on the red carpet running to the platform's edge, acknowledging the still cheering crowds which were held back at the station entrance by barriers manned by the King's guard. Tarlenheim and I were positioned several yards behind the royal couple, apprehensive and alert. For security reasons there was no other person on the platform.

At last we heard the train's whistle and then the great steaming monster swept into the station. In clouds of steam it slid to a halt, miraculously lining up the royal carriage to the red carpet. As the steam dispersed Tarlenheim and I exchanged brief, tense glances. Words were unnecessary, for we both knew what the other was thinking.

As arranged, the Queen and Rassendyll retreated a little at the train's arrival, Flavia several steps behind Rassendyll. After some moments of waiting, the door of the royal carriage opened and there appeared the King of Bohemia. The crowd cheered and waved in response as he stepped down on to the red carpet. He smiled at this noisy, but warm, welcome, but the smile quickly vanished, to be replaced by an expression of shock and disbelief.

He had seen Rassendyll.

While he gazed speechlessly at him, Sherlock Holmes emerged from the train on to the platform only feet away from Rassendyll. The crowd reacted wildly with cries of incredulity. It was a remarkable scene: Sherlock Holmes and Rudolf Rassendyll facing each other, to all but the expert eye mirror images of the Ruritanian monarch. Had I not been aware of the two men's real identities, I would have found it impossible to say which of them was which.

For a long moment it was as though time stood still. The spectators, after initial expressions of query and wonder, were struck dumb as their brains tried to fathom some rational explanation for this surrealistic tableau.

Even Tarlenheim and myself, who had been expecting this confrontation of the two Rudolfs, were temporarily caught up and mesmerised by the scene. The appearance of Rupert of Hentzau at the carriage door broke the spell for me and acted as my cue for action. I slipped past Queen Flavia towards Holmes and Rassendyll. As I did so, I could see by the expression on Rupert's face that he too was shocked into the mental confusion experienced by all the onlookers.

As I neared Holmes, I thrust out my arm in accusation. 'This man is an impostor – a traitor,' I shouted.

Holmes backed away from me guiltily, desperately looking for a means of escape, but I was quicker than he and I grabbed him before he could run. There followed a brief struggle during which I caught the glint of amused excitement in my friend's eye. Then, with a sweeping blow, I knocked his hat to the floor and pulled the wig from his head.

A cry of disbelief rose from the crowd, but still no-one seemed capable of moving. Now, almost enjoying my part in this drama, I pushed Holmes backwards against the carriage wall and turned my attention to Rupert of Hentzau. Once again my arm shot out in an accusatory gesture.

'That man is the traitor's accomplice!' I bellowed.

This cry finally broke the spell. The crowd roared in anger and pushed forward, attempting to break through the barriers. The guards, equally nonplussed by the swift turn of events, nevertheless remained at their posts as they had been ordered and managed to hold the throng back.

King Wilhelm, rather like a drunken man, staggered away from the scene of the action towards Queen Flavia, as I pulled my revolver from its holster. Without hesitation I fired it directly at Sherlock Holmes. There was a loud report, which echoed like thunder among the high rafters of the station. A bright red moon of blood burst on to the chest of Holmes's tunic; he staggered a few steps and then fell face downward on to the platform.

Hentzau leapt forward, pulling the sword from his scabbard, and lunged at me. I stepped back out of reach of the flashing blade and, before he was able to attack again, Rassendyll was there with his sword to parry the thrust.

'Now, Hentzau, we have a little unfinished business,' said he with some satisfaction, advancing on his enemy.

As the Count turned to face Rassendyll, his eyes blazed wildly and it struck me that only at this moment did he fully realise who his new opponent was. He gave a snarl of anger and thrust with his sword. Rassendyll coolly deflected it and Hentzau fell back a pace before rushing at him again. This time Rassendyll shifted position and reached the traitor's face with his foil, laying his cheek open, before darting sideways to avoid a corresponding blow. A thin streak brimmed red across Rupert's left cheek and, as he touched it with the back of his hand and saw the crimson stain, his fury mounted. His foil flashed fiercely, but Rassendyll deftly parried each murderous stroke.

Although the crowd had fallen silent once again, mesmerised by this contest, it was obvious to me that their support was for Rassendyll – or King Rudolf, as they believed him to be. This was clearly in line with Holmes's planning. I could see why he considered it essential that the 'King' should be the person to challenge Count Rupert directly, showing his strength and power as an able monarch. It must be his victory alone, thus eliminating all challenges to his authority.

Rassendyll was slowly forcing Hentzau backwards against the side of the train and then, as he seemed close to pinning him there, his foot caught in the ruffled edge of the red carpet and he stumbled, allowing Rupert the opportunity to slip sideways out of his reach. The Englishman quickly recovered and followed. Hentzau grabbed a carriage door and flung it open into the face of his opponent, who was caught off guard by this desperate tactic. He swerved to avoid the door which swung back with great force, crashing against the side of the carriage. Although it missed Rassendyll it slammed his foil to the side, knocking it from his grasp. It clattered down on to the platform and slipped beyond reach over the edge.

Rassendyll crouched and made a grab for the errant sword, but it was too late. My heart leapt into my mouth as I saw Rupert spring forward to attack the unarmed man. Sensing danger, Rassendyll dived sideways, but not quickly enough. Rupert's sword caught his arm and sliced through his tunic to the flesh. A spurt of blood gave evidence of a deep wound.

Tarlenheim rushed forward and tossed his own sword towards Rassendyll. 'Your Majesty, finish the traitor with my sword,' he roared, much to the delight of the crowd.

Rassendyll caught the weapon and parried swiftly, catching the over-confident Rupert off guard and pinking his shoulder. Rupert gave a cry of pain and backed away rapidly. The tide had turned and he was now facing defeat. He looked about him for some way of escape, but each end of the platform was barricaded and manned by guards. Then suddenly he turned to Rassendyll with that habitual cold sneer on his lips.

'Well, Your Majesty, I will have to take note of an old English adage,' he cried mockingly. 'It is one which I am sure you know. "He that fights and runs away, may live to fight another day." '

With that he turned on his heel, sprinted a short way down the platform and snatched open a carriage door, disappearing inside the train. Rassendyll sped after him, but, as he reached the carriage door, Rupert suddenly reappeared there, his face strangely white and his eyes glazing in a fixed stare. He staggered down the steps into the arms of Rassendyll, revealing a dark stain on the back of his tunic.

Seconds later the Commander appeared in the doorway. In his hand was a sword, glistening red with the traitor's blood.

Chapter Nineteen
Explanations

The events of that day in the Central Station at Strelsau are forever etched in my memory. In moments of reverie I find them filling my mind unbidden with a vivid, almost theatrical, quality to them, as though one had witnessed some kind of nightmare pantomime in which real swords and real blood were used. If it were a pantomime, my friend, Mr Sherlock Holmes, had not only stage-managed the whole production, but had taken a leading part in the drama, including playing a most effective death scene. His totally convincing demise was exactly as he had planned it. As I fired my revolver, filled with blanks, at him, Holmes had clapped his hand to his chest, breaking a small phial of red dye concealed in the lining of the white tunic. As he "bled" from his "fatal wound", he had fallen to the platform with a strangled cry: it was a performance worthy of Sir Henry Irving. Eventually his "corpse" was removed to the Palace, where it made a remarkable resurrection.

In the meantime, after the initial confusion and furore that followed the death of Rupert of Hentzau, the state visit had gone ahead, more or less as planned. Before he left the station I attended to Rassendyll's wound, dressing it with a makeshift bandage. Although the cut was deep, the blade had not severed an artery and no serious damage had been done.

The news of Rupert's treachery and the valiant part played by Rudolf in his dispatch had quickly spread through the city, bringing out even more crowds to cheer the State Coach as it progressed to the Palace with the 'King' and Queen and their rather shaken royal visitor.

At the same time as the dramatic events were being enacted in Strelsau, the King's men, following Tarlenheim's orders, had made lightning raids on the Blues' various strongholds, including the Castle of Zenda and the main garrison at Berenstein. By nightfall the remnants of the Blues who had not been either killed or imprisoned fled the country. Effectively the organisation had been destroyed.

That evening there was a banquet at the Palace in honour of King Wilhelm. The increased joviality and liveliness of the occasion was, it would be fair to say, more to do with Rudolf's triumph and the death of the traitor than the presence of the Bohemian king.

After the festivities had come to an end Queen Flavia, Rassendyll and Tarlenheim visited the private rooms where Holmes and I were preparing for our departure. Warm sentiments were expressed by all.

Flavia took my friend's hands in hers. 'I cannot find words enough to thank you, Mr Sherlock Holmes. You have miraculously banished all dark clouds that loomed over our realm.'

She leant forward and kissed him on the cheek. I have seldom seen my friend as disquieted and at a loss for words as he was at that moment. To save his embarrassment, the gracious lady turned to me. 'And you, Doctor Watson, deserve our thanks also.' She offered me her hand which I took and kissed.

'It was a pleasure, ma'am.' said I.

Holmes turned to Rudolf Rassendyll. 'What destiny for you now?' he asked.

'My destiny has been carved out for me, I think. Fate led me to play the part of the King of Ruritania three years ago and now it would appear that I have no choice but to resume the role.'

'We are to be married in an hour's time,' Flavia interposed quietly. 'My faithful Fritz is to be our best man, but we should take it as an honour if you will both attend the ceremony.'

'It will give us the greatest pleasure,' replied my friend warmly. He laid his hand on Rassendyll's shoulder. 'Colonel Sapt said you were fitted to be King. I am not given to religious musings, but it seems to me that you were in some way born to rule this land. I know you will govern it well and bring stability to the monarchy.'

'I shall do my best.'

'That is all any of us can do, eh, Watson?'

We exchanged smiles.

* * *

Later that night in the small Palace Chapel of St Stanislaus, the Archbishop of Strelsau officiated at the private marriage ceremony of Queen Flavia of Ruritania and Rudolf Rassendyll. Holmes, Tarlenheim and I were the only others present.

In the dim light of candles this man and this woman whom the fates had brought together in love and tragedy sealed their union forever in the exchange of rings.

Ruritania had found its true King at last.

After the ceremony Tarlenheim opened champagne and we toasted the happy couple. Then, at a sign from King Rudolf, he brought forward a velvet-covered box. From it the King removed two gold chains on which were suspended shining gold medals, each shaped like a four pointed star with a white diamond at its heart.

'As my first act as King of Ruritania,' said Rudolf, 'I wish to bestow on you both the highest decoration of my country, the Star of Ruritania. My wife and I and my kingdom are forever in your debt.'

He slipped the chains over each of our heads in turn, saluting us with a kiss on either cheek in continental fashion as he did so. It was a moving moment and we both uttered inadequate words of gratitude.

*   *   *

By morning, having made our final farewells, we were once more on board a train, this time heading westwards for England.

'Well,' said Holmes, at ease and puffing on his pipe, when we had settled down in our carriage, 'as long as the Elfberg dynasty lasts this is one adventure with which you will not be able to regale your readers.'

'Indeed no,' I said, 'although I will write it down for my own personal record. Therefore I should be obliged if you could clarify a few details for me.'

Holmes laughed. 'Good old Watson. No matter what upheavals we experience, that tidy nature of yours exhibits itself. Very well, ask away.'

'To begin with there is something that has been puzzling me for some days. When we were drugged at the British Ambassador's residence, just before you lost consciousness, you made a reference to "new boots".'

'I did indeed. If you recall, Watson, there was something about Sir Roger's story that disturbed me. I could not quite put my finger on the inconsistency and, when I did, it was too late: I had drunk the drugged brandy. He had told us that, after receiving Mycroft's telegram alerting him to our arrival, he had gone to the station to meet us and yet, while telling us this, he was wearing shining new boots without a speck of dust on them or any sign of wear. Obviously he had not left the premises that morning: therefore he was lying. I was just too slow in coming to that conclusion.'

'If you were slow, I was even slower.'

'Ah, yes, but to be fair, you have always had difficulty in translating what you observe into material for deduction. I make my living doing so.'

I knew that protest was futile, so I moved on to a further point. 'Were you sure you would impersonate the King before we even reached Ruritania?'

'Before we left Baker Street! I reasoned that if he had been impersonated previously, he could be so again – this time by me. It seemed that Rupert would always be able to hold the threat of Rassendyll's impersonation whatever the outcome of his current machinations. The only way to deal with this was to scotch the snake altogether. To accomplish this I had to provide a third Rudolf the Fifth. That was why I was determined to keep hold of my travelling bag at all costs – it contains my make-up kit which was essential to my plans.'

'Really, Holmes, this is amazing – that you worked all this out before we left London.'

'There is no point in tackling problems without making some contingency plans. However, it would be wrong of me to lead you to believe that every detail was worked out precisely beforehand. I naturally assumed that I would meet King Rudolf personally and therefore be able to base the disguise on my observations of him. His untimely death caused unexpected problems. However, all's well, eh, Watson?'

'Now that Rassendyll is King, what do you intend to tell Lord Burlesdon about his brother?'

'I have a letter here for him from Rassendyll,' replied Holmes, tapping his breast pocket. 'It confirms that he is well and happy, but, for reasons that cannot be divulged, he can never return to England. Although the message is, in some ways, sad, it should convince Lord Burlesdon that his brother is out of danger, and content with his lot. Now then, Watson, are there any further points you wish to raise before I indulge myself in a little nap?'

'I must confess,' said I, moving on to another point about which I was not satisfied, 'that I found your deductions which led you to believe that Rassendyll was held prisoner at the fishing lodge less than convincing.'

'Really?' said Holmes in mock surprise, suppressing a smile before laughing out loud. 'Hoist with my own petard,' he ruefully said. 'I have to admit, Watson, that my deductions were somewhat flimsy and, for the most part, it was an intelligent guess.'

I stared.

'Yes, yes, I know I never guess – but on this occasion I did. Now shut your mouth, my dear Watson, before you catch a fly.'

Holmes's explanation had left me speechless. It was the only time in our long association together that he admitted to guessing: and yet he had been right. It led me to believe that Sherlock Holmes had turned even guesswork into a fine art.

*   *   *

Thirty-six hours later two weary travellers alighted from a cab in Baker Street. It was good to be back in our old quarters again. Late that night, as we sat around the fire sipping a night-cap, inevitably we fell into discussion of the Hentzau affair.

'The situation we left behind is hardly the ideal solution – an impostor King continuing the Elfberg line, but the alternative was certainly one which we could not condone. Moreover, when all's said and done, he is an Elfberg, after all,' remarked Holmes.

'Love, loyalty and intelligence, all of which Rassendyll possesses, easily make up for any deficiencies of lineage he may hold,' said I.

'Watson, you are still a romantic at heart.' Holmes smiled and stared into the flames. 'However, in this instance, old friend, I believe you may be right.'